Sinis strode over to Theseus. ˻... ˼ girdle and put it on a tree stump. Then he and Theseus began circling each other.

"I Sinis!" cried Sinis. "I bend you double like pine tree!"

"I'm king of the ring!" Theseus shouted back. "You'll bow down to me!"

"I pine bender!" roared Sinis.

"I'm captain of the Troezen Turkeys!" yelled Theseus. And he began to strut around, making gobbling sounds.

"You think you pin me to ground?" said Sinis.

"No!" called Theseus. "That would be too easy! I'm going to tie you to a pine tree!"

"You and who else?" said Sinis.

Enough trash talk, already. I wished they'd get down to wrestling.

Sinis suddenly rushed at Theseus. He picked him up and tossed him high into the boughs of a pine tree, as if he weighed no more than a pinecone. The neck of Theseus's robe caught on a branch, and he dangled high in the air.

"I Sinis!" cried the big bully. "You gonna get it now!"

BOOK · MYTH-O-MANIA · FIVE

Stop That Bull, THESEUS!

By
Kate McMullan

Illustrated by
David LaFleur

VOLO

HYPERION
New York

Text copyright © 2003 by Kate McMullan
Illustrations copyright © 2003 by David LaFleur
Volo and the Volo colophon are trademarks of Disney Enterprises, Inc.

Printed in the United States of America
First Edition
1 3 5 7 9 10 8 6 4 2

ISBN 0-7868-1668-6

Library of Congress Cataloging-in-Publication Data on file.

Visit www.volobooks.com

For Jacob, Matisse, Zachary, and Annie La Fleur

Thanks to my editor, Catherine Daly, for her
heroic efforts on this text, and to Lisa Holton,
Angus Killick, Tara Lewis, and Maria Padilla
at Hyperion

Prologue

You know me, right? King Hades, Ruler of the Underworld. By day, I oversee my kingdom. I make sure the ghosts of the dead get their fair shake in the afterlife. But by night, I sit at my godly computer, typing away, trying to set the record straight on the Greek myths. I hardly have a minute to myself, but that doesn't matter. I'm driven to bring the truth to light. It pains me, it really does, that generations of you mortals have read *The Big Fat Book of Greek Myths* and trusted that you were getting the real story. But thanks to the tinkering of my little brother Zeus, nothing could be further from the truth.

Zeus is lucky he's immortal, because he couldn't tell the truth to save his life. He's the original myth-o-maniac— (old Greek-speak for "big fat liar"). So when he got his big fat hands on *The Big Fat Book of Greek Myths*, it's no wonder the stories turned out to be riddled with *myth-takes*! Look at what he did to the story of the mortal hero, Theseus. Go on, read it straight from the source:

The mortal Theseus vowed to slay the Minotaur, a monster, half man and half bull. In the labyrinth maze, Theseus found the Minotaur surrounded by piles of skulls and bones. He sprang at the monster and killed him with his bare hands.

Lies, lies, lies! There were no skulls, no bones. Theseus went into the labyrinth, all right. But the only thing he did in there was get good and lost. He never killed the Minotaur. Zeus made that up so that everyone would think the Minotaur was gone for good and forget about the monster. You see, Zeus was into building a dynasty. He married dozens of beautiful goddesses, nymphs, and mortals so he could have hundreds of good-looking gods, goddesses, and heroes as descendants. But when one of his grandsons was born with a bull's head, Zeus went *bull*-istic. He wanted to do away with the Minotaur, get rid of him forever. But he knew his daughter, the little bull-boy's mom, would never stand for that. So he did the next best thing. He got rid of the Minotaur by rewriting the myth and saying that Theseus killed him. Bull hooey!

The truth is, Theseus was a bold, brave hero. But he brought new meaning to the words *I forget*. He couldn't remember to put on his sandals unless someone was at his side to remind him to buckle up. All too often, that someone was me. I can't count the number of times I picked up his sword when he left it lying on the ground. Or went back to get his wrestling girdle—old-speak for "belt"—when he left it on top of some rock. You think Theseus remembers? Fuggeddaboutit! But I do—every bit of it. So here's the whole lowdown on Theseus. Just remember where you heard it first—from me, Hades.

Chapter 1

TERRI-BULL WRESTLERS

WELCOME TO THE FIRST
UNDERWORLD WRESTLING FEDERATION
MATCH, FEATURING ALL–GHOST WRESTLERS!

So read the huge red-and-gold banner inside Dead Center, the Underworld wrestling stadium and sports complex. My godly heart beat with pride as I sat in my custom-made seat—upholstered in red leather with a Necta-Cola cup holder—and looked up at that banner. The Underworld Wrestling Federation—UWF—had been my idea. So had the all-ghost matches. My kingdom is filled with ghosts. I figured they'd turn into huge fans, rooting for their favorite ghost wrestlers.

"Wait till you see these wrestlers, P-phone," I said to my bride, Persephone, who sat beside me. "They're so big and strong. They'll knock your socks off."

"I don't wear socks, Hades," Persephone said. "Ever!"

Persephone is into fashion, but she isn't into wrestling. Me? I pretty much live for the sport. I don't like to brag, but a few centuries back, I represented Team God in wrestling in the very first Olympic Games. After a while, the training got to be too much, so I gave it up. Now I was looking forward to being a major UWF promoter.

I leaned forward in my seat to see the Furies, my Underworld avengers. They were sitting down the row from Persephone, their big, black wings folded snugly against their backs in the stadium seats. I was sorry to see that their snaky heads were bent over *The Hot Times*, the Underworld newspaper. I knew they weren't wrestling fans. They'd never even been to a match. But I'd gotten them primo seats for this big opening event. Couldn't they at least *pretend*?

"*Pssst,* Tisi! Meg! Alec!" I called to them. "What do you think?"

Tisi glanced up, her glowing red eyes wide. "What, has it started?"

"I meant the stadium," I said. For this event, I'd gotten a huge glob of burning tar from Tartarus, the fiery part of my kingdom. I'd hung it from the stadium ceiling. It didn't smell too great, but it lit the place with a eerie, flickering light. I thought it was a great special effect.

"Very nice," said Tisi, clearly unimpressed.

"The first match will make wrestling history," I promised. "Neither wrestler has ever been in the ring before. But you can tell from looking at them that they are going to be HUGE. Hey, I know. How about you Furies root for Spook, and I'll take Phantom?"

"Okay," said Tisi. "So tell me the rules."

"There aren't many," I said. "One wrestler tries to pin the other wrestler to the mat for the count of three. However they do it is pretty much okay."

Tisi nodded. Then she started reading her paper again.

That really bugged me. If she had to read, couldn't she at least read the wrestling program I'd bought for her? It had a cool photo of Yulio the Spook, one of my brand-new wrestling phenoms, on the cover. The Furies spend their nights flying up to earth, avenging the sins of the wicked. Most days, they sleep. So you'd think they'd appreciate being invited to an exciting daytime event like the inauguration of a brand-new wrestling federation. But evidently something in the news was far more riveting.

Finally, I couldn't stand it any longer. "What's the hot news, Furies?"

"There's a crime wave up on earth," Tisi said.

"Three big bullies are ambushing travelers on the Troezen—Athens Road," added Meg.

"They are *bad*!" said Alec. "They *rob* mortals!"

"Then they do away with them in the most horrible ways." Tisi shuddered.

"If only a mortal would fill out a Furies Action Request Form," said Meg.

"Then we could fly up to earth and *whip* them!"

said Alec, fingering the little scourge that hung from her girdle.

"But the victims never live to tell about it," said Tisi. "And their relatives are too scared of the bullies to fill out the form."

"It's awful, Hades," Persephone added. "Look." She opened the newspaper to a map. A stretch of the Troezen–Athens Road had been marked with three big Xs. The Xs showed where the three big bullies lurked, waiting for unsuspecting mortals to come along.

"Terrible," I said. "Hey, look, the stadium lights are flashing. The match is about to begin!"

"Specters and spectators!" the announcer called. "Welcome to the Underworld Wrestling Stadium! Pro wrestling, move over. Here comes the Underworld's first all-protoplasmic wrestling event! Tonight, we have two soon-to-be champion wrestlers. Yulio 'The Spook' . . ."

The crowd cheered for Spook as he floated down the aisle wearing a blue cape. He levitated over the ropes, landing noiselessly in the ring. The fans went wild.

"... and Alexi 'The Phantom!'" the announcer said.

Phantom drifted down the aisle in a white cape. The ghosts cheered like crazy.

"Go, Phantom!" I called, hoping Persephone and the Furies would start rooting for Spook. But they didn't seem to get the idea.

The bell dinged. Right away Spook lunged for Phantom. But Phantom rose quickly over his head.

The ref blew his whistle. "No floating!"

"Sorry," muttered Phantom, drifting back down. "Listen, can we start over?"

The ref rolled his eyes. "All right."

The bell rang again: *Ding!*

Now Phantom tried to belly-bust Spook.

Spook flattened himself on the mat, screaming, "No! Don't hurt me!"

I couldn't believe it. Was this some sort of comic opener, with wrestling clowns?

"Get up and wrestle!" yelled the ref.

"Don't shout!" wailed Spook, looking as if he might burst into tears. "I'm new at this!"

I heard a low noise rising up from the stands.

What was it? It grew louder. And then I knew. It was the sound of thousands of ghosts, booing.

I didn't blame them. This match was a disaster.

"What is wrong with them?" I muttered.

"Don't you worry, Hades," Persephone whispered. "It's just the first match."

But the second match—Shadow vs. Walking Dead—was worse. All those two did was wail and moan. The boos from the crowd were deafening.

Tisi giggled. "Where did you get these ghostly wrestlers, anyway, Hades?"

"I found them wandering in the Asphodel Fields," I said. "I know, I know. It's the place for ghosts of mortals who weren't too good or too bad in life. But look at them. They've got great muscle-shaped protoplasm. I thought they had what it takes."

"Why didn't you go to Tartarus?" asked Meg.

"Where the really *bad* ghosts go!" said Alec.

"I tried that," I explained. "But the ghosts down there are punished with burning flames and flaming tar." I shrugged. "Five minutes of that, and they lose their fighting spirit."

Ding! The third match started. Undertaker vs. Zombie.

Don't ask.

Ghosts began leaving the stadium mid-match. Several wafted past my seat, moaning about wanting their money back.

"Go to the box office," I told them. "Full refunds for everyone."

That cheered them up.

But I slumped down in my seat as the stadium emptied out. "UWF is a disaster," I moaned.

"Oh, Hades," said Persephone. "Did you ask these ghosts what they did in life before you signed them up for the UFO?"

"UWF," I muttered. "And no, I didn't ask. Why?"

"It might make a difference," said Persephone. "I'll bet you didn't even read their bios in the program."

"P-phone, you know how busy I've been," I began.

"Listen, Hades," Persephone said. And she began reading from her program. "'On earth, Yulio was a pet sitter. He enjoyed making small catnip toys for cats.'"

"A pet sitter?" I said.

Persephone nodded and began reading again. "'Alexi was head librarian in Thebes.'"

"A librarian?" I was horrified. "But you saw his muscles, P-phone. The guy was buff!"

"Books are heavy, Hades," said Persephone. "Shall I read more?"

"No! Stop! I get the idea. Oh, why did I ever think I could pull this off?"

"Don't have a cow, Hades," said Tisi. "When the next mortal wrestling champ comes down to your kingdom, all you have to do is sign him up *before* he gets judged. That way, he won't get sent to Tartarus."

"Maybe." I shrugged. "But the MD—Mortal Division—has never really caught on in earthly wrestling," I told Tisi. "It's never been able to compete with the Wrestling Immortals—Cyclops, Python, the Calydonian Boar, Scorpion. They're the champs. But none of them will ever die, so they'll never show up in my kingdom. I need big, bad, powerful mortals who aren't afraid to fight. Tough, mean mortals. But where am I going to find mortals like that?"

Tisi shrugged as she folded up her newspaper.

That newspaper. It gave me an idea.

"Let me see that map again, will you, Tisi?" She handed it to me, and I looked at those three big Xs on the Troezen–Athens Road. "That's it!" I exclaimed, thumping the map with my hand. "I'll go up to Troezen tomorrow. I'll find those three big bullies. And I'll give them a choice. After they die, they can either go straight to the flaming punishment fields of Tartarus. Or"—I grinned—"they can sign a contract to spend their afterlives wrestling in the UWF!"

Chapter II

BULL-HEADED THESEUS

First thing the next morning, I opened my magic wallet. It had been a gift from Persephone and was monogrammed with the initials K.H.R.O.T.U.— King Hades, Ruler of the Underworld. I tossed in an Ambrosia Power Bar, a shaker of Ambro-Salt, and a VI-pack of Necta-Cola. Now I'd never be without the food of the gods. (We gods need to eat ambrosia and drink nectar daily to keep our godly good looks.) The magic wallet grew large to hold the items. Once they were inside, it shrank back to its original size, and I slipped it into my robe pocket. I stuck in some wrestling contracts, too.

Persephone walked me out to my chariot. "Be careful, Hades," she said.

"Don't worry, P-phone. I'm immortal, remember?"

"Still, those bullies sound very dangerous," said Persephone. "I don't want you getting hurt."

"Fat chance," I said. I kissed her good-bye.

"Arf! Arf! Arf!" I looked down to find my three-headed pooch, Cerberus. "Sorry, boy, boy, boy," I said, leaning down and scratching him under his chins. "I swear I wasn't going to leave without saying good-bye to you, too."

I galloped up to earth and parked in the usual lot outside of Athens. On with my Helmet of Darkness—*POOF!* I vanished. Then I chanted the astro-traveling spell, known only to us gods. *ZIP!* I was instantly transported to Troezen.

I landed in the woods just outside of the city. A dekafoot or so away from me was a huge rock. Beside it stood a young man wearing a wide brass wrestling girdle. A champ! He looked like a mortal. Was he a candidate for the UWF? The girdle was decorated with the head of a strange-looking bird. What kind was it? I couldn't tell. Next to the young man stood a woman who had to be his mother. I decided to stick around for a while, to see what they were up to.

"You are sixteen now, Theseus," said the mom. "I told you what would happen when you turned sixteen. Remember?"

Theseus scrunched up his face, thinking hard. At last he said, "I forget."

"I said I'd tell you the truth about your father," said his mom.

"Right, right." Theseus nodded. "Who is my father?"

"You'll be surprised," said his mom. "It is King Aegeus of Athens."

"A king!" said Theseus. "Wow!"

"He had to leave Troezen to rule Athens before you were born," she went on. "But before he left he hid a sword and a pair of golden sandals under this rock. He said he hoped one day he might have a son strong enough to lift the rock."

It was a whale of a rock.

"If you can lift the rock and get the sword and sandals," his mother went on, "you may travel to

Athens to claim your place as the king's son. Can you lift the rock, Theseus?"

"Of course I can!" said Theseus.

"Go on, then," said his mother. "Lift the rock."

"No!" said Theseus. "Lifting the rock would be too easy."

Easy? Theseus had big muscles. If he really huffed and puffed, he could probably boost the thing a tiny bit. But no way would it be easy.

"Theseus, don't start with that 'too easy' nonsense," warned his mother.

"I want to be a hero like Hercules," Theseus said. "So I must never take the easy way!"

"That rock weighs a dekaton, Theseus," said his mother. "Lifting it won't be easy."

Theseus drummed his fingers on his chin. "What would Hercules do?" he mumbled. "I know!" he exclaimed. "He would lift the rock with his big toe."

"Oh, I see where this is going." His mother sighed.

"So that is what I will do!" Theseus immediately sat down on the ground. He stuck the big toe of his right foot under the rock. I watched, fascinated, as the young mortal struggled to lift the rock with his toe. The veins in his neck popped out. His face turned red. But that rock stayed put.

Just then, I sensed a movement in the bushes. I turned in time to see a figure with blue-streaked hair duck behind a tree. Only one god was into streaking his hair—my little brother, Poseidon. Invisibly, I tiptoed over to see. Yep, there was Po, peeking out from behind the tree. Why was he spying on Theseus and his mother?

"Po!" I whispered.

"Huh?" Po looked around, confused.

"It's Hades," I said. "I'm right beside you. I've got my helmet on. You can't see me. What are you doing here?"

"Just wanted to be here when the kid lifted the rock," Po whispered. "Can't believe he's trying to do it with his toe."

We both looked back at Theseus. He was still grunting and groaning. His mother, meanwhile, had made herself comfortable under a shady tree. She was doing a crossword puzzle. Obviously, she knew her son wasn't going to give up any time soon.

"Come on, Hades," said Po. "I'll tell you

everything." He led the way down a hill to a stream a good distance from the big rock.

I followed and sat down on a fallen tree beside him. I took off my helmet. *FOOP!* I reappeared. As we dangled our feet in the clear water, I told Po how I'd come to earth looking for some down-and-dirty mortal wrestlers. Then Po told me his tale.

"You know I've always been a let-the-good-times-roll kind of god," he began.

"Always," I agreed.

"But once, I was ready to give it all up for a mortal," he went on. "For Aethra, actually—Theseus's mother."

"No kidding," I said.

Po nodded. "It was nearly seventeen years ago now. Aethra and I had spent a few wild evenings together in Troezen. I was head-over-heels in love, Hades. To make a long story short, one night we had a little too much bubbly and ended up at the Troezen Speedy Wedding Chapel."

"You married her?" I said, surprised.

Po nodded. "For the first time ever, this old party god was ready to settle down."

"So what happened?"

"Everything was great for a couple of weeks," said Po. "Then King Aegeus came through town. To be polite, we invited him over. He'd just come from the oracle of Delphi. He told us the sibyl had given him a strange warning. She told him not to open his wineskin until he reached the highest point in Athens or he'd die of grief. Aethra loves sibyls," Po went on. "So she started telling King Aegeus about prophecies she'd gotten over the years. I was bored out of my mind. Then suddenly I realize Aethra is totally flirting with the guy. He was old, Hades. His hair was already gray! But next thing I know, King Aegeus has totally forgotten about the sibyl's warning. He whips out his wineskin and starts pouring drinks for himself and Aethra—didn't even offer me one. And Aethra is like, 'Get lost, Po!' She jilted me for a mortal, Hades! Me, Poseidon, King of the Seas!"

"That's awful, Po," I said. "I'm sorry."

"I was a wreck for almost a week. But what can you do?" Po shrugged. "Aegeus didn't stick around long. Had to go rule Athens. But Aegeus and Aethra think that Theseus is Aegeus's son. What a joke!"

"You mean he's *your* son?" I said.

"Look at him, Hades. He's mine, all right. And I keep track of him. That's why I'm here today. I knew Aethra would bring him to lift the rock on his sixteenth birthday." He stood up. "Let's go and see if the kid's made any progress."

The two of us made our way back up the hill. Po ducked behind the tree again. I put on my helmet—*POOF!*

Theseus was still at it. His face had gone purple. I didn't want to think what color his toe might be by now. But the rock hadn't moved. Aethra was dozing in the shade.

"Chip off the old block, eh?" said Po.

"He does look like you, Po," I agreed. "He definitely has your chin."

"He's stubborn, though," Po said, watching the poor mortal strain and grunt. "Must get that from his mother."

I rolled my eyes. "Listen, Po, I have to go find those big, bad bullies. Great to see you."

"Wait, Hades," said Po. "How about giving the kid a little help before you go?"

"You're his dad," I pointed out. "Why don't you help him?"

"I'm not invisible," Po said. "But you are. Come on, bro! You know he could lift the rock if he did it the normal way."

"Oh, all right." Why was saying a simple *no* so hard for me?

I made my invisible way toward Theseus. I took hold of the rock with both hands and lifted it slightly.

"Yes!" cried Theseus. "I have lifted the rock!"

"You're kidding!" Aethra jumped up to see. "Well, I'll be. Hold it steady, Theseus. I'll reach under it and get the sword and sandals."

"No!" cried Theseus. "That would be too easy!"

But Aethra dove under the rock. She dragged out a dirt-covered sword and pair of sandals.

Theseus lowered his toe to the ground, and I carefully lowered the rock with it.

"Here, Theseus." Aethra handed him the sword and sandals. "When your father sees these, he will know you are his son."

Theseus began wiping sixteen years of grime off

the sword. At last a golden bull's head appeared on the hilt. He wiped off the golden sandals, too.

"I've packed some roast-beef sandwiches in your lunch box," Aethra told him. "A ship awaits you at the coast. You can sail for Athens tonight."

"No!" said Theseus. "Sailing would be too easy." He held up the sandals. "These sandals are a sign that I should walk."

"Walk?" cried Aethra. "Did you forget about the three bad bullies lying in wait along the Troezen–Athens Road? They'll try to rob you and kill you!"

"I will rid the world of those bullies!" claimed Theseus.

"You are so bullheaded!" cried Aethra. "You must have gotten it from your father."

"I don't think so," muttered Po.

Whoever it came from, Theseus was definitely the most bullheaded youth I'd met since I spent a month looking out for my god-son, Perseus. But I liked Theseus's plan for ridding the Troezen–Athens Road of the bullies. It fit perfectly with my own plan for recruiting wrestlers for the UWF.

"I'm going to tag along with Theseus," I told Po. "Why don't you come, too?"

"Can't," said Po. "I have to meet Zeus at the Oracle of Delphi at IV o'clock. He and Apollo are buying the property from Granny Gaia and me."

"You own part of Delphi?" I said. "I never knew that."

"A wide river that runs under the mountain," Po said. "All the world's rivers are mine, you know that. Listen, Hades, do me a favor. Keep an eye on Theseus, will you?"

"I don't know, Po," I said. "Maybe for a day or two." It never seemed to turn out well for me when I agreed to look after other people's kids.

"Thanks, Hades!" said Po. "I knew I could count on you, bro." Then—*ZIP!* He astro-traveled off to Delphi.

I turned back toward Theseus. He was giving his mother a kiss on the cheek.

"Good-bye, Mother!" he said. "I shall meet the big bad bullies on the Troezen–Athens Road. I swear by the hilt of my father's sword that I shall wrestle them to the ground! By the time I reach Athens, I shall be a big-time hero."

Theseus started off down the road.

"Oh, Theseus?" his mother called after him. "Forget something?"

I had to smile. She was holding up his sword, his sandals, and his lunch box.

BIG BAD BULL-Y

I followed invisibly behind Theseus as he started off for Athens. It was a breezy day, fine for walking. Making myself known to mortals when I'm invisible is always awkward. I wanted to get it over with. So we hadn't gone far when I said, "Greetings, Theseus."

"Huh?" Theseus stopped. He whipped out his sword and began slicing the air. "Who said that? Show yourself, coward!"

I jumped back to avoid getting seriously scratched by his flailing sword. "Take it easy, Theseus," I said. "I am Hades, god of the

Underworld. I am about to reveal myself." I took off my helmet. *FOOP!* I appeared before him.

"But I'm not ready to die!" said Theseus. "I have bullies to wrestle!"

"I'm not the god of death," I said as I put my helmet into my K.H.R.O.T.U. wallet and watched it shrink back down to pocket size. "Just ruler of the kingdom of the dead."

"Hold it." Theseus looked at me suspiciously. "How do I know you're a god? Maybe you're one of the big bad bullies."

"No, I'm a god," I told him. "I'm bigger than any mortal. And look. I have a godly glow. Haven't you ever seen a god before?"

Theseus tapped his fingers on his chin. "I forget," he said.

"It doesn't matter," I told him. "Listen, if you're going to Athens, I'll walk with you."

Theseus's face lit up. "Two buddies traveling together? A road trip?"

"Sure," I said. And we started off again. "Nice wrestling girdle," I told him after we'd walked for a while.

"Do you like it?" Theseus grinned. "I was captain of my high-school wrestling team, the Troezen Turkeys." Ah, so that was the head of a *turkey* on his girdle. "I've been wrestling since I was a baby," he went on. "Once I even wrestled a lion! You should see my headlock. Nobody can get out of it. I'll bet even Cyclops would have trouble with it."

"You like Cyclops?" I asked eagerly. I was a major fan!

"Eagle-Eye is the best!" Theseus said.

From then on, the trip sped by. There was so much to talk about! Theseus opened his pack and showed me his Immortals of Wrestling cards. He had Cyclops, of course. Python, the great snake wrestler. Stinger, the scorpion. And the wily Calydonian Boar.

"Actually, I'm here on a recruiting trip for the Underworld Wrestling Federation," I told him, and I explained how I wanted to sign up the big bad bullies to wrestle in the Underworld.

"But I have sworn to wrestle these bullies to the ground!" Theseus frowned. "At least, I think that's what I swore."

"It is," I told him. "How about this: I'll sign them up and then you wrestle them."

"Right!" said Theseus eagerly. "Teamwork on the road trip!"

Theseus was a little intense about the whole "road trip" thing. But I was okay with that.

We walked all morning. Midday, we stopped at a little shish kebab stand outside the town of Mycenae. I sprinkled some Ambro-Salt on the kebab and broke out a Necta-Cola, so I had a complete and balanced godly meal.

We walked on then, heading north. The land grew hilly. By afternoon, we found ourselves trudging up a mountain. It was covered with pine trees.

"What's that about?" Theseus pointed to a pine tree. It had been bent double. A rope held its tip firmly to the bottom of its trunk.

"Odd," I said. But I didn't think too much about it. Mortals are always doing strange things.

We passed another bent-over pine. And another. And another. It was very odd.

"We must be on our guard," said Theseus. "Only

a big bad bully is big enough and strong enough to have bent these trees."

From then on, we kept a sharp lookout. We saw nothing. Then, as we climbed higher, we heard a faint voice crying, "Help! Help!"

"I will save you!" called Theseus. "Where are you?"

"Here!" cried the voice.

We ran through the pine trees toward the voice.

"Help!" it cried. "Save me!"

The voice was so close. We looked around. But we saw no one.

"Down here!" the voice said.

There, close to the ground, was the upside down and very red face of a mortal. It took me a moment to realize that the poor guy had been flipped heels-over-head and tied to the tip of a bent-over pine tree.

Theseus drew his sword. "I shall cut the rope and free you!" he said.

"No! No!" cried the mortal. "Don't cut the rope!"

Theseus frowned as he lowered his sword. "Why not?" he asked. "Would that be too easy?"

"Don't you see?" said the upside-down mortal. "If you cut the rope, the top of the pine will spring up with great force. And I'll spring with it!"

He was right. The way he was tied made the tree a spring-loaded trap.

We heard a terrible shriek and looked up to see a mortal sailing over the treetops.

"See?" said our mortal. "What did I tell you? His rope got chopped. And look what happened to him!"

"Don't worry," I said. "I'll hold the treetop while Theseus cuts you free."

I held the tree so it couldn't spring. But even with all my godly strength, it wasn't easy.

I heard another shriek. And another hapless mortal flew over our heads.

"There!" said Theseus as our mortal flopped onto the ground.

"Oh, thank you! Thank you!" he cried. "Thank you! Thank you!"

Theseus gave the mortal one of his roast-beef sandwiches. The mortal devoured it hungrily, chewing and thanking us all at the same time.

"Who tied you to the tree like that?" I asked him.

"Sinis!" said the mortal.

"And how did you happen to meet this Sinis?" I asked.

"Never met him, exactly," said the mortal. "I was walking along the Troezen–Athens Road. All of a sudden, this huge guy jumps out at me, turns me over, and ties me up. I thought I was a goner!" He looked around nervously.

A chorus of shrieks filled the air now, as mortal after mortal arced through the sky.

"Oh, this is awful!" cried the mortal.

"Sinis is a big bad bully," I told Theseus. "I'm sure of it."

"He's a bully, all right," said the mortal. "Come on. Let's get out of here. He'll be coming to spring me soon!"

"Let him come," said Theseus. "When he gets here, I shall . . ." He looked puzzled. "What was it again?"

"Wrestle him to the ground," I said.

"Right!" said Theseus. "I shall wrestle him to the ground."

"No offense," said the mortal. "But Sinis is big. And strong. *He* could take him." He gave a nod in my direction. "But you don't stand a chance."

"You've never seen me wrestle," said Theseus. "Check out my girdle. It's the Troezen Turkeys Championship—" He stopped. "What's that noise?"

I heard it, too.

Footsteps.

THUMP! THUMP! THUMP!

"Run for your lives!" cried the mortal as he dashed into the forest and disappeared. "It's Sinis!"

Chapter IV

BEEFY JERK

One great thing about being immortal—you never have to run for your life.

I didn't run from Sinis. Theseus stood his ground, too.

THUMP! THUMP! THUMP!

Suddenly, two loops of rope shot through the air, and before we could say "Roped like a pair of steers!"—we were.

"What the—?" cried Theseus. His arms were pinned tightly to his sides.

I, too, was trussed like a Troezen Turkey. A small

flex of my godly biceps would have broken the rope, of course. But I decided to play along and see what happened.

Out from between two pine trees stepped a beefy mortal with bulging muscles. He was nearly god-size. (But that was the only way in which he resembled us gods. We, as a group, are incredibly good-looking, and Sinis was a total troll.) He wore a short robe, which showed off of his hairy tree-stump legs. An ax hung from his girdle. In a gruff voice, he shouted, "I, Sinis! You, quake with fear!"

Sinis held the end of a rope in each hand. Now he raised his beefy hands and twirled the ropes. They wrapped around us from our necks to our waists. He was a whiz with a lasso, I had to give him that.

The giant mortal looked us over. His beady black eyes shone with excitement. "I got two trees just right for you," he said. "Very springy. Send you halfway to Thebes. *Boinnnngg!*" He grinned, showing a large gap between his two front teeth.

"No, Sinis!" said Theseus. "You will not tie us to your trees. For I am Theseus, and I have come to . . . have come to . . ."

"To wrestle you to the ground," I whispered.

"To wrestle you to the ground!" Theseus declared.

"Why wrestle?" Sinis growled. "You lose. You end up on pine tree anyway. *Boinnnngg!*"

"Ever done any wrestling, Sinis?" I asked.

"Wrestle plenty." Sinis nodded. "But always beat other guy to pulp. Boring."

"Wrestle me!" cried Theseus. "It won't be boring, I promise!"

Sinis eyed Theseus. Then he said, "I win, I get turkey girdle?"

"Right!" agreed Theseus. "And if I win? I'll tie you to a pine tree."

Sinis laughed. "You think you make me go *boinnnngg*?"

"I'm no bully," said Theseus. "I wouldn't do that."

"You free." Sinis gave his right-hand rope a yank and Theseus began spinning like a top.

"Hey, no fair!" cried Theseus. "I'll get dizzy!"

Theseus finally stopped twirling. He staggered in a circle trying to slip the last loop of rope off over his head. Finally, he succeeded. He took off his turkey girdle, his sword, and his sandals. He laid them on the ground, and began stretching, limbering up for his match.

Sinis looked over at me. "You stay tied."

"No thanks," I said, and I puffed out my chest, snapping Sinis's rope as if it were a cooked spaghetti noodle.

Sinis's eyes grew wide. He began backing away.

I smiled. What's the fun in being a god if you can't show off for the mortals once in a while?

"I'm King Hades," I told him. "You've heard of me?"

"Hades?" Sinis backed up some more. "I die now?"

"No, no, I rule the Underworld," I said. "I'm not the god of death." I wished these mortals would get that straight. They always think I'm the bad guy.

"Ready to wrestle!" called Theseus.

"Hold it a minute!" I called back. "Remember our deal?"

"Oh, I forgot." Theseus sighed loudly.

"Come here, Sinis." I beckoned him over to a couple of tree stumps. I sat on one and he sat on the other. "I'll cut to the chase," I said. "You're a mortal. Sooner or later, you're going to kick the bucket and end up in my kingdom."

"Long, long time from now," said Sinis.

"You never know. Anyway, the ghosts of the mortals who've been good in life get to live in Elysium, where they party day and night."

Sinis smiled. "Like parties."

"Ghosts of mortals who weren't too good or too bad live in the Asphodel Fields," I went on. "It's like the 'burbs. Lots of shrubbery, but not much happens."

Sinis nodded. "Boring."

"But the ghosts of mortals who've been bad?" I shook my head. "They get sent to Tartarus, where they're tortured by flames and burning hot tar for all eternity."

Sinis furrowed his brow.

"You're a big bad bully, Sinis," I said. "You'll end up in Tartarus for sure."

"Flames?" Sinis looked worried.

"Burning hot," I told him. "Awful. But there *is* something that will save you from Tartarus." I took one of the UWF contracts out of my pocket.

Sinis's black eyes lit up with interest.

"If you sign up to wrestle in the Underworld Wrestling Federation," I told him, "I could fix it so that you don't have to spend eternity in Tartarus."

It was a no-brainer, but Sinis thought about it for a while.

"I'm wai-ting!" called Theseus.

I held up a hand. "Two minutes!" I turned back to Sinis. "You'd have a cool wrestling name. Something like—Sinis 'The Pine Bender'!"

Now Sinis broke into a grin. "Deal," he said.

I held the contract and he made his mark on the dotted line.

"Thanks." I folded the contract and stuck it back in my pocket. "The ghosts in my kingdom will never boo you."

"Boo who?" said Sinis.

"Crying already, Sinis?" called Theseus.

"I never cry!" shouted Sinis.

"I'll make you cry *mama*!" said Theseus.

"Just wrestle, will you?" I gave Sinis a pat. "Go on. Show me your stuff."

Sinis strode over to Theseus. He took the ax from his girdle and put it on a tree stump. Then he and Theseus began circling each other. Sinis had ten dekapounds on Theseus. But Theseus was speedy.

"I Sinis!" cried Sinis. "I bend you double like pine tree!"

"I'm king of the ring!" Theseus shouted back. "You'll bow down to me!"

"I pine bender!" roared Sinis.

"I'm captain of the Troezen Turkeys!" yelled Theseus. And he began to strut around, making gobbling sounds.

"You think you pin me to ground?" said Sinis.

"No!" called Theseus. "That would be too easy! I'm going to tie you to a pine tree!"

"You and who else?" said Sinis.

Enough trash talk already. I wished they'd get down to wrestling.

Sinis suddenly rushed at Theseus. He grabbed him around the middle. He picked him up and tossed him high into the boughs of a pine tree, as if he weighed no more than a pinecone. The neck of Theseus's robe caught on a branch and he dangled high in the air.

"I Sinis!" cried the big bully. "You gonna get it now!"

Chapter V

STAMPEDE!

Theseus reached for a pine branch above his head. He pulled himself up until he was sitting on it. Then he grabbed the trunk, bending the branch way back, and *SPROOONG!* It snapped forward, hurling the Troezen Turkey captain at the Pine Bender.

"Ooof!" cried Sinis as Theseus slammed into his belly.

The bully doubled over, holding his gut. Theseus didn't give him time to recover. He leaped forward, knocking him off his feet. Sinis popped back up. The two of them went at it then, and it was a joy to see.

Theseus had nice, clean moves. Sinis was sneaky and tricky—which made him an excellent candidate for my bad-guy Underworld wrestling team.

At last Sinis ran at Theseus. Theseus ducked, caught him in the middle, and picked him up on his shoulder. He started twirling around.

"Now it's *your* turn to get dizzy, Sinis!" he cried, spinning like crazy. Then he ran over to a bent-over pine tree. He flipped the groggy giant upside down and thrust him into its branches. He grabbed Sinis's own rope and tied him to the tree.

"How do you like it, Sinis?" cried Theseus.

"Not much." Sinis groaned.

"Right," said Theseus. "And how do you like this?" He picked up Sinis's ax from the tree stump, and *WHAP!* He chopped the rope that held the tip of the pine to the trunk.

BOINNNNGG!

"YAAAAAAAAAA!" cried Sinis as he catapulted up into the sky. "YOU SAID YOU NOT *BOINNNNGG* ME!"

"Oh, right," said Theseus, furrowing his brow. "I forgot."

We watched Sinis arc through the sky and begin his descent back to earth.

THUD! He landed somewhere far away.

"One bully down," said Theseus. "Two to go."

As king of the Underworld, I've become an expert on the dead. I was pretty sure this big bad bully could never have survived his *boinnnngg.* I made a mental note to phone Charon, who ferries the ghosts of the dead across the River Styx to my Kingdom. I'd ask him to watch for a big beefy mortal named Sinis. I'd tell him not to send him to be judged, but to put him up in the wrestling stadium until I got home.

Theseus swung Sinis's ax again and hacked off a branch of the tree that had catapulted the bully into the air. "I shall call this the Pine Bough of Theseus!" he declared, waving it about. "Come, Hades. We can hike to the top of this mountain by nightfall." He started walking.

Theseus had taken his pine bough. But he'd left behind his turkey girdle, his sword, and his sandals. I picked them up and put them into my K.H.R.O.T.U. wallet. It shrank back down and I pocketed it. Then I caught up with Theseus and we continued up the mountain.

It was a long trek, and very steep. Being a god, I could simply have astro-traveled to the top, no drosis—old Greek-speak for "god sweat." But foolish pride made me walk. I didn't want Theseus thinking that I, Hades, took the easy way.

At dusk, we reached the mountain top.

I heard a voice. It came from someplace not far from where we stood.

"You think that's smooth?" the voice said. "It's rough as sandpaper!"

Theseus and I made our way through the trees to a clearing. It dropped off to a steep cliff at the far end. There, sitting on a rock at the very edge of the cliff, was another giant mortal. This one was bald. A smaller mortal knelt before him, washing one of his giant feet.

"Put a little muscle behind that pumice stone!" shouted the giant. "Exfoliate! I want my foot as smooth as my head!"

"I'm trying, Sciron!" wailed the smaller mortal. And he began scrubbing harder.

"Looks like we've found another bully," Theseus whispered to me.

I nodded. Sciron was definitely a bully. He'd probably force the little mortal to paint his toenails, too.

"Now the other foot!" cried the giant. He yanked one big foot out of the wash basin and plopped in his other foot. "See that callus?" he barked. "Get rid of it!"

"Yes, Sciron," said the mortal. He started pumicing up a storm.

In a loud voice, Theseus said, "Greetings, Sciron!"

"Huh?" Sciron jumped up, knocking over the wash basin. "Who said that?"

"I, Theseus! I have come to . . . to . . ."

"Wrestle you to the ground," I whispered.

"Wrestle you to the ground!" yelled Theseus.

"Fat chance," scoffed Sciron. His giant blue eyes landed on me. "Who are you?" he boomed.

"King Hades," I told him.

Sciron gasped. "You . . . you mean I'm croaking? My time on earth is up?"

"No," I said from between gritted teeth. Clearly

I needed to hire a mortal P.R. agent to clear this matter up! "I'm *ruler* of the Underworld."

"And you are a big bully," Theseus told Sciron.

"Who says so?" Sciron eyed the little mortal. "You, squirt? Did you tell him I was a bully?"

"Oh, no, not me, Sciron!" said the little mortal. "I'd never say that!"

"Good." Sciron folded his massive arms across his chest. "Because if you did, you know what I'd do?"

"Yes, Sciron!" said the mortal. He began to shake so violently that he dropped the pumice stone. "You would . . ."

With that Sciron bent his right leg at the knee. Then with his huge and powerful foot, he kicked the poor mortal.

WHACK!

"Yiiiiii!" shrieked the mortal as he sailed high in the air.

"That's the CCCLXVIIIth mortal I've kicked off the cliff this month," boasted Sciron.

Theseus and I rushed to the edge of the cliff. A giant turtle was paddling in the sea below. As the mortal fell, the turtle swiftly swam toward him. His huge jaws sprang open.

The mortal splashed into the sea inches from the turtle.

SNAP! The turtle's jaws caught only sea spray.

The lucky little mortal swam for his life toward the shore. The turtle swam after him, but the little mortal was too speedy, and the turtle gave up. He looked at Sciron, giving the bully a nasty, reptilian glare.

"Don't worry, Tank!" Sciron called down to the turtle. "You won't go hungry! I've got another mortal here to wash my tootsies!" He turned to Theseus. "You!"

"Why should I?" asked Theseus.

"Come on! You'll get a kick out of it!" Sciron chuckled at his joke. "Or are you too scared?"

"I fear nothing!" cried Theseus.

"Then scrub my feet," said Sciron.

I checked out Sciron's feet. Ugh! They were the nastiest feet I'd ever seen, by far. He had bunions and hammertoes and thick yellow calluses. Clearly all that kicking took a toll.

"I won't scrub your feet!" said Theseus. "That would be too easy."

"Easy?" said Sciron. "Have you ever tried to smooth a callus? It's far from easy!"

"Really?" said Theseus. "Is it nearly impossible?"

"Absolutely," said Sciron. "Even with a good pumice stone, hardly anyone can do it."

"All right," said Theseus. "I shall scrub your feet. But first, I have vowed to . . . to . . ."

"Theseus has vowed to wrestle you," I told Sciron. "Have you ever done any wrestling?"

"I was ultraheavyweight champion of my nursery school," bragged Sciron. "I was first in the Giant League in Junior High. I was—"

"I get the picture," I told him.

Sciron turned to Theseus. "Foot wash first," he said. "Then wrestle."

"Two difficult tasks!" Theseus smiled. "You're on."

I elbowed Theseus. "Remember our agreement," I said.

"What agreement?" said Theseus.

"You can start scrubbing," I told him. "But let me do the talking."

"Any time now!" Sciron called to Theseus.

Theseus knelt down and began scrubbing Sciron's left foot.

"Sciron," I began, "do you have any idea what happens to bullies after they die?"

Sciron grinned. "They become ghost bullies!"

I nodded. "Your ghost will come down to my kingdom. It will be tortured forever and ever with burning hot flames."

"The hotter, the better!" cried Sciron. "I fear nothing!"

"Another bully told me that once," I told him. "And now I fall asleep at night listening to his screams."

Sciron looked a little less sure now.

"However, there is one thing that could save you," I told him. I waved a UWF contract in front of his face. "If you sign up to become a big bad wrestler in the Underworld, I could keep you out of the flames."

Sciron thought for a moment. "Would I have a cool wrestling name?" he asked.

"Definitely. How about Sciron 'The Kickmeister'?"

Sciron grinned. "Where do I sign?"

I held out the contract. Sciron signed it. I folded it up and was putting it into my pocket when I saw that Sciron was slowly, slowly bending his right knee, pulling back his foot. He was getting ready to kick Theseus off the cliff!

I opened my mouth to shout a warning to Theseus.

But I was too late.

Sciron swung his leg forward in a mighty kick.

Chapter VI

BULLY DOZER

Theseus saw Sciron's kick coming. In the nick of time, he dove out of the way.

But Sciron had swung his leg so powerfully that the momentum flipped the giant bully upside down and sent him spinning over the cliff.

"*YIIIIII!*" cried Sciron as he tumbled through the air.

Once more Theseus and I ran to the edge of the cliff.

Below, Tank's turtle eyes grew wide as the giant hurtled toward him. He didn't open his jaws. Sciron was too big for a gulp. Instead, Tank quickly paddled until his broad back was directly under the falling bully.

SPLAT!

The bully belly-flopped onto the giant turtle's shell.

"Ooooh . . ." groaned Sciron.

Tank seemed to smile as he began swimming with the bully on his back.

Sciron managed to sit up. "Watch it, Tank," he said. "Don't tilt. You know I can't swim. Take me to shore. Tank? To shore! Why are you swimming this way? Shore is that way. Tank? TANK?"

Theseus and I watched as Tank carried Sciron far out to sea. Slowly Sciron's cries faded away. I wondered what would happen to the big bully now. Nothing good, it seemed. Again, I made a mental note to call Charon. I had to tell him to keep an eye out for a big bald bully.

Theseus picked up the stone he'd been using to scrub Sciron's feet. "I shall call this the Pumice Stone of Theseus!" he cried. "Come Hades! Time for us buddies to be back on the road!" He began marching down the far side of the mountain.

This time our hero had forgotten the Pine Bough of Theseus. I picked it up, put it in my wallet, and hurried down the hill after him.

"Two bullies down," Theseus said when I caught up with him. "One to go."

Two wrestlers signed with the UWF, I thought. One to go. We'd had good luck with the first two bullies. I hoped our luck would hold for number three.

Theseus and I made our way down the mountain, stopping only for a fast supper. Theseus said he'd share his roast-beef sandwiches with his road buddy. That was me. I took one, sprinkled on some Ambro-Salt, and had a meal fit for a god. I was sorry I couldn't share a Necta-Cola with Theseus, but giving godly food or drink to a mortal is a big no-no. After our meal, we walked on through the pine woods. By the time we reached the bottom of the mountain, it was growing dark. To our surprise, we saw a large, lit-up dwelling ahead.

In those days, it was the custom for travelers to knock on any door at sundown and ask to be fed and for a bed for the night. When we gods came to earth, we did it all the time. It was considered extremely rude for mortals to say no.

"I wonder if the owner of that house up ahead will take in two weary travelers," I said.

"I don't know," said Theseus. "But let's ask if we can stay there, too."

"I meant us, Theseus," I said. "We are weary travelers. Say," I added, peering at the house, "is that a sign on the roof?"

It was. As we got closer, we could read what it said: PROCRUSTES PALACE HOTEL.

"What luck!" I exclaimed. "A proper place to rest."

When you knocked on a random door, you never knew whether your bed would be lumpy or if they'd be serving boiled worms for supper. Proper hotels were rare, and I felt fortunate that we'd stumbled onto one.

"I have no money for a hotel," Theseus said. "But perhaps the innkeeper will let me do some incredibly difficult task to pay for my stay."

We drew closer to the hotel. Signs were plastered all over the building:

TRAVELERS WELCOME!

COME IN! THE DOOR IS ALWAYS OPEN!

NO MONEY? NO PROBLEM!

OUR BEDS ARE JUST THE RIGHT SIZE FOR YOU!

Theseus's smile faded as he read the bit about NO MONEY? NO PROBLEM. "Maybe the hotel manager will have an incredibly difficult task for me anyway," he said.

We walked up to the entrance. There were no guests lolling about on the porch. A sign on the door said OPEN. We went inside. The lobby was empty except for a mortal in a sparkling white tunic who was dozing behind the front desk.

"Ahem!" Theseus cleared his throat.

The mortal jumped up. He quickly smoothed back his glossy coal-black hair, which was perfectly parted down the middle of his head.

"Welcome, guests!" he exclaimed. "Good evening! I am Procrustes, hotel proprietor, at your service." He bowed. "Please, would you be so kind as to sign my guest book?"

"We have been traveling all day," said Theseus as

he signed his name. "We could keep going, of course. That would not be too hard for us. But when we saw your hotel, we decided to give you the honor of housing us for the night."

"Oh, you won't be sorry. . . ." Procrustes tilted his head to read the name upside down. "Thee-see-us. At this hotel, we offer many unique services to our guests. I am proud to say that I, personally, tuck all my guests into bed for the night." He smiled, showing a row of perfectly white teeth. "So, Theseus, are you ready to go nighty-night?"

"I am not one bit tired," said Theseus. "But I will rest for a few minutes." Suddenly, his face fell. "Oh, darn," he muttered.

"What's wrong?" asked Procrustes.

"I, uh, forgot something," Theseus muttered. "Something I like to have when I go to sleep."

"Is it a teddy bear?" asked Procrustes.

Theseus's eyes widened. "How did you know?"

"Come now. You can't possibly think you're the first guest to forget a teddy, can you?" Procrustes shook his head. "No, happens all the time. That's why I keep a spare on hand."

"But it won't be Fee-Fee," said Theseus sadly.

"That's true," said Procrustes. "Nothing can replace your beloved Fee-Fee. But little Fuzzy is quite a charmer." He took a key from the hook. "Room I is vacant." He gave me a wink and mouthed *Be right back!* Then he took Theseus's arm and began leading him down a hallway. "Come and take a look. My, you're a tall young man. But I have a feeling you're going to fit into my little bed just right. And then, nighty-night!"

I saw that Theseus had left his pumice stone on the check-in desk. I added it into my wallet. Then I took a seat in one of the lobby chairs, thinking again how lucky we were to have stumbled on a hotel. A hotel in the middle of nowhere on the Troezen–Athens Road. I hadn't even known there was one. It was sort of funny, when I thought about it. A big hotel. No sign of any other guests. Procrustes seemed very welcoming. Maybe a little *too* welcoming. *No money? No problem?* That was unusual. And was it a little weird that he tucked all his guests into bed himself? I began to feel uneasy and decided to take a look around. I headed down the hallway, stopping outside Room I. That's odd, I thought. In the whole hallway, there was only one door. The door to Room I. I put my ear to it.

"I love a good hard test!" I heard Theseus saying. "This is a test, right, Procrustes? To see if I can escape? That's why you're tying me to the bed, right, Procrustes? Procrustes?"

Chapter VII

BULLWHACK!

I slammed my godly shoulder into the door of Room I.

BAM!

The door flew open. I stared into the room. There were two beds. Nothing else. One bed was very, very long. The other was very, very short. Theseus was tied to the short bed. His legs and feet stuck out at the end. In one of his tied-down arms he held a worn brown teddy bear.

"It's polite to knock," said Procrustes. He stood above Theseus, holding an ax.

"Stop!" I cried. "Put down the ax, Procrustes!"

"I can't," he said. "Then I wouldn't live up to my promise, would I?"

"What promise is that?" I asked.

"You saw my sign," said Procrustes. *"Our beds are just the right size for YOU!"*

"But this bed is way too small for Theseus," I said, keeping an eye on that ax.

"Exactly," said Procrustes. "So clearly I must make him fit the bed!"

He raised the ax higher. He was about to bring it down on Theseus's legs. I leaped forward and yanked it away.

"So you are a big, bad bully, Procrustes," I said. "I had no idea."

"No one ever does," said Procrustes, sitting down on the long bed. "I just don't fit the bully stereotype. I get away with murder because I'm polite and neat as a pin."

"That could work in the ring," I muttered to myself as I bent down to untie Theseus.

"No!" Theseus cried as I started undoing the first knot. "Do not untie me! What would Hercules do if he were here? He would untie the ropes himself. So that is what I will do."

"Oh, I assure you, you'll never get free," said Procrustes. "When I tie a knot, it stays tied."

"You mean your knots are impossible to untie?" asked Theseus.

"Precisely," said Procrustes.

"Here, I'll untie you." I bent over him again.

"No, Hades!" cried Theseus.

"Hades?" Procrustes blinked and looked up at me, wide-eyed. "The god?"

"The one and only," I told him.

"Oh, good heavens!" said Procrustes. "You mean my time on earth is up?"

"No!" I snapped. "You're mistaking me for Thanatos. *He's* the god of death. I'm king of the Underworld. Strictly a ruler. Nothing to do with who dies or when."

"Whew!" said Procrustes, patting his chest in relief.

On the short bed, Theseus grunted with the effort of trying to untie the ropes. He wasn't making much progress.

"One day your life on earth will end, Procrustes," I went on. "Do you have any idea what awaits a bully like you in my Underworld kingdom?"

Procrustes frowned. "I am sure it is less than delightful," he said. "For this reason, I haven't given it much thought, really."

"I don't blame you," I said. "It's nothing but punishment with burning hot flames and flaming hot tar."

Procrustes shrugged. "I have a high pain tolerance," he said. "I can bear almost anything for a while. How long does this punishment last?"

"For all eternity," I told him. "Every morning you get up and—you're toast."

"One hand is freed!" called Theseus from the little bed. "Oops! Never mind. That rope was tied to the bear."

Procrustes sat mulling over his fate. Then he looked up at me. "Is there nothing I can do to escape these eternal flames?"

"That depends," I said. "Ever done any wrestling?"

"Certainly," said Procrustes. "I was on a semi-pro team for a while. Traveled to matches all over Greece. My roommate was an extremely tall fellow. Wherever we went, he complained that the bed was too short for him. Every night, he whined about it. I couldn't get a decent night's sleep with all his bellyaching, so one night I told him I could make it so he'd fit into bed perfectly. He fell asleep, I got an ax and *WHACK!*" Procrustes smiled, remembering. "I got such a bang out of it that after a while I quit wrestling so I could whack full time."

"Yes!" cried Theseus. "My left arm is free!"

"Why the extra-long bed?" I asked Procrustes. "Do you get many freakishly tall guests?"

"No, no, no," said Procrustes. "It didn't seem fair for me to whack only tall folks. So the long bed is for the shorties. I stretch them to fit that bed. It's very simple, really. I tie their arms to the head of the bed. Then I tie ropes to their ankles and attach them to a pulley system. After a day or so, *voilà!* The bed fits. And once again, Procrustes Palace Hotel lives up to its promise."

"I did it!" cried Theseus, jumping out of the short

bed. "I have untied dozens of impossible-to-untie knots!"

"Excellent work, Theseus," said Procrustes. He turned back to me. "Why did you ask about wrestling, King Hades?"

I took another wrestling contract from my pocket and made Procrustes an offer.

"No flames or hot tar for the UWF wrestlers," I told him. "Just cheering fans. I'm thinking we could work the beds into your act," I added. "Maybe bill you as 'Mr. Nighty-Night' Procrustes."

"Show me the dotted line," said Procrustes. "And I shall show you my signature."

It was a done deal.

"Now, Procrustes," said Theseus. "Get ready to rumble!"

"Ah, let's do have a go at each other," said Procrustes. "Ready when you are, Theseus."

I acted as the referee while Theseus and Procrustes wrestled. Each time Procrustes put Theseus in a headlock or slammed him to the floor, he apologized for any pain he might be causing. Several times, Theseus came close to pinning

Procrustes. But Procrustes always managed to slither out of the hold and flip Theseus over onto his back. Late in the match, Procrustes held Theseus down and bent one of his legs up in the air. It looked like a pin to me.

I started counting: "I! II!"

But before I got to III, Theseus wrenched his shoulders from the floor, grabbed one of Procrustes's legs and one of his arms, and before you could say "Our beds are just the right size for YOU!" he tied the big bully into a knot and tossed him onto the long bed.

"No, no! Not on the bed!" shrieked Procrustes. "There's something I forgot to tell you about—"

Suddenly the head of the bed rose up and slammed down on the foot of the bed.

BANG!

Chapter VIII

STEAK-OUT

No sooner had the long bed snapped shut like the jaws of a giant sea turtle than a trap door sprang open under it. *WHOOSH!* The bed disappeared down the black hole and a second later we heard a faint splash.

Slowly, slowly the bed rose up from below. When it opened, it was empty.

I shook my head. "So that's how Procrustes got rid of his poor victims."

Theseus and I left the Procrustes Palace Hotel. I stopped at the entrance and flipped the OPEN sign to CLOSED.

Once we were outside, Theseus held up Fuzzy. "I

shall call this the Teddy Bear of Theseus!" he proclaimed.

"Fine," I told him. "Listen, Theseus. I've got what I came for." I patted my pocket, which held three signed wrestling contracts. "I'm going back to the Underworld now."

"You're joking, right?" said Theseus.

"Well, um . . ." I scratched my head. "Not really. Is it a problem?"

Theseus put his hands on his hips. "I thought we were two buddies on a road trip."

Oh, the old road trip again.

"We were," I agreed. "And now one of the buddies—me—is taking off."

"You can't take off in the middle of a road trip!" said Theseus. "Maybe we took care of the three bad bullies. But there are still adventures to be had. Buddies don't desert each other!"

It wasn't worth arguing about. Another day or two on the road is nothing when you're immortal. Besides, I had most of Theseus's stuff in my K.H.R.O.T.U. wallet. If I gave it to him now, he'd be too weighted down to walk to Athens on his own.

"I see your point," I told him. "Let's go."

Theseus put Fuzzy under his arm and we started off for Athens. The nearly full moon lit our way. My buddy Theseus and I walked on the Troezen–Athens Road for another day. We weren't attacked by thieves. Or bullies. The only adventure we had was when we were attacked by mosquitoes.

The following morning we reached Athens and found ourselves in the marketplace. It was packed with Athenians buying fish, grape leaves, goats, and such.

"Okay, buddy," I said to Theseus. "Athens. End of the road."

Theseus socked me in the shoulder in a manly sort of way. "I must make myself known as a hero. And you must go back to your kingdom. Here is where we part. Take care, good buddy."

Theseus turned and walked toward the center of the marketplace.

"Hold it, Theseus!" I called after him. "You forgot these!"

I opened my K.H.R.O.T.U. wallet. I took out his turkey girdle, his sword, his sandals, his pine bough, and his pumice stone. I handed them to him.

Theseus put on the sandals and the turkey girdle. He tucked the sword, pine bough, pumice stone, and teddy bear into his girdle. He looked like a deranged peddler.

"And listen, Theseus," I added, "when you tell of this road trip, no need to mention me." I didn't want anyone to know I'd been hanging out with a mortal. It would ruin my reputation as the fearsome ruler of the Underworld.

"Farewell, Hades," said Theseus. "Until we meet again."

"Farewell, Theseus!" I took out my Helmet of Darkness and put it on. *POOF!*

I was curious to see how Theseus would make himself known to the Athenians. So instead of astro-traveling right back to my chariot, I stayed and watched.

Theseus was a natural self-promoter, and he wasted no time. He went to the highest point in the marketplace and jumped up onto a wine barrel.

"Attention, shoppers!" he called to the crowd. "I am Theseus!"

"Are you giving out free samples?" called a shopper.

"I have just traveled the Troezen–Athens Road!" Theseus shouted.

"Big deal!" another shopper shouted back.

"We've all done that!" shouted another.

"What's with the teddy bear?" shouted still another.

A crowd was gathering. They might not know who Theseus was or what he was up to, standing on that barrel. But obviously they thought he might provide some entertainment.

"I have just rid the road of the three big bad bullies!" Theseus proclaimed.

"Oh, bull!" shouted a shopper.

"Yeah!" shouted another. "You and what army?"

"I did it alone!" Theseus called. "With my bare hands!"

Good boy! I thought.

"The first was Sinis, 'The Pine Bender'!" cried Theseus. "From him I took the Pine Bough of Theseus!" He pulled it from his girdle and waved it over his head.

"Yay!" called the crowd, which was growing bigger by the minute.

"The second was Sciron 'The Kickmeister'!" cried Theseus.

"Yes, yes!" called the crowd.

"From him I took the Pumice Stone of Theseus!" He plucked it from his belt and tossed it into the crowd. There was a great scramble as mortals dove for it.

"I got it!" cried one, holding it up. "Lucky me!"

Theseus was a natural crowd pleaser.

"The third was . . . uh . . ." Theseus frowned.

He'd been doing so well. I couldn't let him look like a forgetful fool. So I quickly astro-traveled to his side and whispered, *Procrustes!*

"Procrustes!" cried Theseus. "Mr. Nighty-Night! From him I took the Teddy Bear of Theseus!" He bent down and handed it to a small girl in the front row.

"Awwwwww!" cried the crowd.

"The three bullies are history!" cried Theseus. "They will trouble you no more!"

"Three cheers for Theseus, the hero!" cried a bystander. And the crowd began to cheer.

When the cheering died down, an Athenian called, "Tell us of your deeds, brave Theseus!"

"Yes, tell us!" cried another.

I smiled. Theseus had done what he set out to do. He had made himself a hero in Athens. He began telling of his heroic deeds.

It was time for me to go. I'd just started chanting the astro-traveling spell when I spied a winged chariot approaching from the east. I stopped mid-chant.

The chariot dipped lower. It was drawn by a pair of winged serpents. They had black-and-green stripes and large neck ruffs. The crowd looked up and saw the chariot, too.

"Queen Medea," several of them murmured nervously as the chariot approached. The serpents landed not far from where Theseus stood.

A woman stepped out of the chariot. She had jet-black hair with a bright green streak that matched her serpents. She wore a black robe.

I saw that her aura glowed with a faint green light. That meant she wasn't a mortal. But she didn't have the rosy glow of a goddess, either. so I figured her for some sort of a low-level sorceress. I got a bad feeling as she began walking toward Theseus. I didn't trust her.

"Crowd, disperse!" Medea commanded, waving a hand in the air.

Muttering, the disappointed Athenians went back to their shopping.

Medea turned to Theseus. "You must be Theseus," she said. "Welcome to Athens."

"Thanks." Theseus jumped down from the wine barrel.

"So you have rid the Troezen–Athens Road of the bullies," Medea said.

She must have been lurking close by to have heard what Theseus had told the crowd.

"It is true," said Theseus. "With my bare hands."

"Well done," said Medea. "Why don't you come and dine at the palace tonight? I know when my husband, King Aegeus, hears of your deeds, he will want to thank you personally. And to welcome you to Athens as a hero."

"I accept!" said Theseus. "What time's dinner?"

"VI o'clock," said Medea. "What a fine sword you have." She reached out and touched its hilt.

"Decorated with the head of a bull. My husband the king told me he once had such a sword."

"This is that very sword," said Theseus. "For King Aegeus is my father."

Medea gasped. "No!"

"Yes," said Theseus. "He left Troezen before I was born, but he hid this sword under a great rock. On my XVIth birthday, I lifted the rock—with my big toe—and pulled out the sword. And these golden sandals, too." He gestured toward his sandaled feet.

"I love those!" said Medea. "Well! King Aegeus will be pleased to find out that the new hero of Athens is also his son!" She smiled, but I sensed that underneath she was smoldering with hatred for Theseus. "Say, I have an idea!" she said. "Let's surprise your father tonight."

"Surprise him?" Theseus frowned. "What do you mean?"

"Don't tell him who you are right away," said Medea. "Wait and let him discover who you are by your sword and your sandals. That way your presence will please him all the more."

"Then I shall do it!" said Theseus.

"Oh, and tonight at dinner?" Medea went on. "You will meet your half-brother, my little son, Medus."

Uh-oh. Medea had a son. No wonder she didn't like Theseus. With him around, little Medus was no longer first in line for the throne.

Theseus didn't pick up on this. He only said, "I will teach him how to wrestle. It is never too early to learn."

"Until tonight, then," said Medea. "Oh, by the way, do you eat steak?"

Theseus said, "Can't get enough of it."

"Good!" said Medea. "I shall prepare a special one for you tonight!" She turned and walked swiftly back to her chariot. She gave a command. Her serpents spread their wings and took to the air, leaving a trail of green smoke.

Theseus hopped back up onto the wine barrel. "Now, where was I?" he said, as the crowd quickly gathered around him once more.

"You found a man tied to the tip of a bent-over pine tree!" shouted out a woman.

"Sinis, 'The Pine Bender'!" said Theseus, and started in where he'd left off.

I left him to entertain the crowd while I astro-traveled to the palace. It was a big white stone structure perched on the edge of the highest cliff in Athens. I went inside and made my invisible way to the kitchen. Just as I suspected, Medea was there. And she was alone, which meant she'd kicked out all the palace cooks.

"Dum-de-dum," Medea hummed happily to herself as she stood at a counter, chopping and mixing together herbs and pastes and liquids. Every now and then, she consulted an ancient-looking cookbook. Finally she crumbled some dried leaves into the mixture and poured it over a big hunk of beef.

"There!" Medea covered the steak with a cloth. "It's marinating!"

She dipped her hands into a water bowl and washed them. Then she waltzed out of the kitchen, still humming.

I walked over to the steak. I lifted the cloth. I sniffed. Whatever she'd put in the marinade had an odd smell. Medea's cookbook still lay open on the counter. I glanced at her recipe. It was called Steak Take-Out. Strange name. My eye swept down the list of ingredients: fish paste, squid ink, octopus slime. Nothing unusual so far. I kept reading: crushed thorns, nettles, dandelion fluff, wolfsbane. Wolfsbane! That was the odd smell. Wolfsbane grew on the hills outside Athens. Any wolf that nibbled it fell instantly to the ground, dead. Then it hit me like a dekaton of toxic beef. Medea wanted to use the steak to take out Theseus. She wanted to poison him!

Chapter IX

WHERE'S THE BEEF?

Theseus strode into the packed banquet hall that night. Everyone cheered. I was right behind him, but I had my helmet on, so no one caught my entrance.

It's never a good idea for a god to meddle much in mortal affairs. I wasn't going to step in unless I absolutely had to. But Theseus was in terrible danger. So I stood by to protect him, just in case.

"Welcome, Theseus!" King Aegeus said in a voice that trembled with age.

"Thank you, sire," said Theseus. The servants showed him to the place of honor between King

Aegeus and Queen Medea. Theseus sat down. I hovered invisibly behind him.

The table was spread with tasty-looking appetizers. I was hungry. But I wasn't about to eat anything Medea might have made. True, I'm immortal. Poison can't kill me. But wolfsbane would give me a god-size upset stomach.

Before anyone could take a bite, Medea stood up. She said, "A toast to Theseus!"

Everyone at the table jumped up. They raised their glasses high.

"To Theseus, who has rid the land of Greece of three bad bullies!" said Medea.

"Here! Here!" said the old king and all the retainers and royal hangers-on at the table. They tossed back their wine and sat down.

"To Theseus!" said Medea.

Everyone jumped up again. The ancient king struggled to his feet.

"To our hero, who has made our roads safe again!" said Queen Medea.

Everyone tossed back another glass of wine and sat down.

"To Theseus!" said Medea.

Everyone jumped up once more.

"Zeus's pajamas!" muttered the old king, tottering up again. "This is hard on the knees."

I saw what Medea was up to. She wanted everyone to be woozy with wine. That way when Theseus fell to the floor, poisoned, everyone would think he'd simply had too much vino.

I rushed invisibly to the door where the servants stood waiting for the toasts to end so they could bring in platters of food.

"Dinner is served!" I announced loudly.

The servants paraded in, everyone sat down, and that was the end of Medea's toasts.

"The queen ordered this dish especially for you," a servant said as he put a brass platter with a smoking hot steak in front of Theseus.

I stood behind Theseus, ready to knock the beef away before he could take a bite.

"Mommy!" cried Medus, Medea's little son. "How come I don't get a special steak?"

"Shhh, Medus," said Medea. "Eat your hummus."

"I want steak!" shouted Medus. "Now!"

"Silly boy," said Medea. She turned to Theseus. "Eat! Shall I cut your steak for you?"

"No!" said Theseus. "That would be too easy. Watch! I shall slice it with my sword."

Theseus was impossible! I hovered behind him, ready for action.

Theseus jumped to his feet. He drew the sword from his girdle. He held it over the smoking steak and— Chop! Chop! Chop! Chop! Chop! He cut it into chunks. He speared a chunk with the tip of his sword. He opened his mouth wide. Looking like a sword-swallower from a circus, he brought the tip of the sword toward his mouth.

My elbow was ready to swat the sword away.

But King Aegeus suddenly cried, "My sword!" His trembling hand reached for the weapon, accidentally knocking it out of Theseus's hand. "My son!" He rose and threw his arms around Theseus.

Everyone at the table cheered. Everyone but Medea. She was steaming.

"What's that funny smell?" said Medus. "Eww! Look at the steak!"

The meat was now a nasty shade of green. It had eaten through the copper platter.

"Zeus's pajamas!" cried the old king. "That steak was poisoned with wolfsbane. Guards!"

The palace guards ran into the banquet hall.

"Find out who fixed this steak and bring them to me!" ordered King Aegeus.

"Excuse me a moment, dear," said Medea. She took Medus's hand and stood up.

"No!" Medus pulled away from her. "I'm hungry! I don't want to go!"

Just then the guards brought the cook into the banquet hall. She pointed at Medea.

"The queen prepared Theseus's steak herself," the cook said. "She's the one you want!"

Instantly Medea surrounded herself and her son in a thick cloud of green smoke. When it lifted, they had vanished. Moments later, flapping wings sounded, and we all knew that Medea and Medus were fleeing in the serpent–drawn chariot.

"What a nut case." King Aegeus dabbed at his face with his napkin. "Good riddance."

Now the servants cleared away the poison steak

and brought in heaping platters of mussels, squid, and octopus. Everyone feasted and celebrated the great deeds of Theseus.

I snagged a few mussels. Even without Ambro-Salt, they were excellent!

Theseus was out of danger now. My promise to Po to look after him had been more than kept. So I chanted the astro-traveling spell, and *ZIP!* I was on my way back home.

To some, the Underworld is a dank, sunless swamp. But to me, it's home sweet home.

As always after I'd been gone for a while, I found problems waiting for me. Persephone was having the den wallpapered in a floral print. Ghost workers aren't very reliable, and she was totally stressed. I caught Hypnos, my first lieutenant, snoozing on the job—three times in one day! He *is* the god of sleep, but if he wants to work for me, he has to keep his eyes open.

The biggest problem, however, was my own fault. I'd forgotten to phone Charon and tell him to keep an eye out for the three big bullies. Their ghosts had shown up in my kingdom, all right. But they'd gone straight into the court system like any other ghosts. I hired a crack team of underworld lawyers from the ghostly firm of U. O. Plenty to see if I could keep them from being sent to Tartarus. (The fees those greedy ghosts charged me? Don't ask.) I was up to my ears in paperwork. The trials, appeals and so forth stretched on for a couple of years.

Meanwhile, the UWF was on hold. Oh, I had some of my mortal friends up at Wrestle Dome in Thebes scouting big bad wrestlers for me. And sometimes, when Persephone was up on earth to bring in the spring, she'd call and tell me about a promising meanie. So my talent pool was growing. But my three big bad bully stars were unavailable. And until I could get them into the ring, I didn't want to start the UWF up again.

One morning I was in my chariot, heading over to the courthouse to attend yet another hearing on the matter, when my phone rang.

"It's Po," said the frantic voice on the other end. "Emergency! You gotta help me out, Hades."

Chapter X

A LITTLE BULL

"I'll help you, Po," I said before I thought better of it. Why could I never say no?

"Theseus is in trouble," said Po.

"I thought he was safe in Athens."

"Was, bro. Was. But the kid got bored hanging out with the old king. He's hardwired to have adventures, Hades. Just like his old man. So last week when the ship showed up to take XIV Athenian youths to Crete, Theseus hopped on board."

"He'll like Crete, Po. It's got great beaches."

"Theseus didn't go for a vacation, Hades. He's

gone to do the impossible. He's gone to slay the Minotaur!"

"The who-otaur?"

"Minotaur," said Po. "Terrible monster. Body of a human with the head of a bull."

"Bullheaded," I said. "Like Theseus."

"Ha-ha, Hades. But this is no time for a joke. Here's the deal. King Minos of Crete used to sacrifice these really splendid bulls to me."

"Minos. Is he related to King di Minos who runs the pizzeria down in my kingdom?"

"Yeah," said Po. "Very close relative. Anyway, a while back, sacrifice time rolls around. You don't have mortals sacrificing to you, Hades. So maybe you don't know that it's not like in the old days, when we gods got to eat all the meat from the sacrifice. We only get the cooking smoke now. The mortals get the meat. But, hey, a nice aromatic smoke is excellent. Anyway, I'm looking forward to some very fine smoke from King Minos's primo hunk of beef. But when the smoke shows up, it's barely a whiff."

"What happened?"

"Minos sacrificed this really stunted little bull to

me, Hades. Old as the hills, too. It was the *worst* sacrifice ever! So I asked around, and I found out that the bull Minos was going to sacrifice to me was such a fine specimen that at the last minute, he decided to keep it for himself."

"Uh-oh." If there's one thing we gods hate, it's mortals who think what's good for the gods is good for them. Big mistake.

"*Uh-oh* is right," said Po. "I couldn't put up with that! I thought that if King Minos liked bulls so much, I'd give him a little bull. So with some help from this sorceress I met at a beach party, I arranged for Minos's wife, Queen Pasiphae, to give birth to a baby with the head of a bull."

"That wasn't nice, Po!" I said.

"Give me a break, Hades. So anyway, Queen Pasiphae loved her little Minotaur baby. But every time King Minos saw him, he totally freaked. And Zeus went nuts when he heard about it too. Pasiphae is one of his daughters, which meant that Zeus had a grandson with a bull's head."

"Ha!" I said. "I'll bet he was furious when he found out what you did, Po."

"Yeah, well, he doesn't exactly know it was me," said Po. "So don't go blabbing to him, Hades. Anyway, when the Minotaur got to be seven or eight, he started bellowing and galloping around the palace and butting the furniture with his horns. Zeus came for a weekend visit, and he was horrified. He ordered Minos and Pasiphae to get rid of the little bullheaded guy. Pasiphae stood up to her dad and said, 'No way.' Then Zeus said, 'Then hide him so that no one will ever see him again.' So Pasiphae went to see Daedalus. He's the famous architect who designed their palace at Knossos. Built himself a little penthouse right on top of it. Amazing guy, Daedalus. You've heard of him, right?"

"Not really. Go on."

"So Pasiphae and Daedalus put their heads together and decided to make a labyrinth—a gigantic maze—for the Minotaur to live in. It's huge, Hades. It's got thousands of passageways going in all different directions. Once you're inside, it's impossible to find your way out again."

"My phone battery's running low, Po. What's your point?"

"Take it easy, Hades. I'm getting there. So Pasiphae sent the Minotaur to live inside the labyrinth. Everything was okay for a while. Then, when he was around nine years old, the Minotaur started bellowing and making a huge racket. Seems that when he got older, his monstrous side took over. He was hungry and he only wanted one thing to eat: humans."

"Hold it. Bulls eat grass."

"Not this one. So Minos had to figure out a way to get the Minotaur some humanburgers, and he remembered this old grudge he had against the city of Athens. Minos sent a ship with black sails to Athens and ordered King Aegeus to put fourteen Athenian youths and maidens on board and send the ship back to Crete. There, they would be fed to the Minotaur. Minos said that if Aegeus didn't do it, he'd send his army to destroy the city."

"Oh, boy."

"So Aegeus sent the youths and maidens," Po went on. "The Minotaur ate them, and that was the end of it. Or so everyone thought. Then, nine years later, the Minotaur got all riled up again. It's the same story. He's hungry, but he'll only eat humans. So Minos sent the black-sailed ship to Athens again. And fourteen more young people were sent to feed the monster. And now, nine years later, it's happened again. But this time, Theseus kicked one of the youths off the ship and took his place. He's one of the XIV!"

"Why don't you send a storm to blow the black-sailed ship off course, Po? You can keep it from ever getting to Crete."

"By the time my Sea Nymph Intelligence Team let me know what was happening, it was too late for that. The ship should be entering Knossos Harbor about now. You've got to get there right away, Hades. You've got to stop Theseus from going into the labyrinth!"

"One question, Po. Whose son is Theseus?"

"Mine."

"Right. So why don't *you* get to Knossos right away and save him?"

"I *want* to. But I can't. Not now. I'm begging you, bro. I'm smack in the middle of this Delphi real estate deal. If I miss a single meeting, Zeus will fix it so that I end up with zilch."

That I could believe. But still. What did he think I was, the god of baby-sitting? No!

But before I could object again, Po said, "Theseus *is* your nephew, Hades. Listen, I'm counting on you, big bro. Theseus is in over his stubborn head this time."

I was about to say no, I wasn't going. Me, the original yes-god. But Po cut me off.

"And be careful, Hades. Strangers aren't welcome in Crete. I hear King Minos has some crazy new security system on the island. It's this giant—"

"Giant what? Po? Are you there? Listen, this isn't a good time for me. I'm in the middle of this lawsuit and . . . Po? Say something!"

But he didn't. He couldn't. My phone battery was as dead as the citizens of my kingdom. Now I had no way to tell Po I wasn't going. And here he was counting on me, his big brother.

I sighed. "Come on, Harley. Let's go, Davidson." I pulled on the reins and turned my steeds in the direction of my shortcut up to earth. "We've got to take a little trip."

Chapter XI

BULL HOOEY!

Once on earth, *ZIP!* I astro-traveled to Crete, arriving in the late afternoon. I landed close to Knossos Harbor. Sure enough, the black-sailed ship was just docking. I stood at the side of the road in a crowd of Cretans, watching it pull into its berth.

"Stran . . . ger . . . on . . . road!" an odd metallic voice cried out. "Stran . . . ger . . . on . . . road!"

I looked around. There, coming toward me was a giant bronze robot! The thing was at least four dekafeet tall. What a monster! A large leather pouch was strapped to its chest. Its metal legs clanged as it strode down the road toward me, calling, "Stran . . . ger! I . . . den . . . ti . . . fy . . . your . . . self . . . now . . . or . . . Ta . . . los . . . pelt . . . you . . . with . . . rocks."

The robot must have been what Po meant when he said Minos had a new security system.

The robot reached into his pouch, grabbed a rock, and heaved it at me.

There was only one thing to do. I put my helmet on and *POOF!* I disappeared.

"Ta . . . los . . . make . . . stran . . . ger . . . go . . . a . . . way," said the robot. "Ta . . . los . . . good . . . at . . . job."

Big robot body, little robot brain. Still, Talos was impressive.

Suddenly, a terrible clattering noise filled the air, followed by a vicious roar.

"There's our Minotaur again!" said a mortal standing not far from me in the crowd.

"He sounds hungry!" said another.

"Roaring for his supper," said a third.

"And here it comes!" said the first mortal, pointing to the black-sailed ship. "Look!"

The Athens XIV—VII young women and VII young men—began walking down the ship's gang plank. I was too far away to tell who was who, but the last one down waved eagerly to the crowd. Had to be Theseus. A guard guided them directly into an open cart. A pair of black bulls began pulling the cart toward Knossos.

Cretans lined the road. As the cart passed by, they jeered at the unlucky XIV.

"Hey, Minotaur chow!" one yelled.

"Bull bait!" yelled another.

The cart rolled by me. Most of the victims hung their heads sorrowfully as the Cretans taunted them. But not Theseus.

"I am going into the labyrinth to meet this Minotaur!" he shouted to the crowd. "I shall wrestle him to the ground and slay him! He shall never eat human flesh again!"

The Cretans cracked up. "Oh, right!" they yelled.

"I shall slay the Minotaur!" cried Theseus as the cart clattered by. "And I won't do it the easy way, either, with a sword or a cudgel. No! I shall do it with my bare hands!"

"Bull hooey!" yelled one of the Cretans. And he hurled an overripe tomato at Theseus. *Splat!* It hit him on the shoulder.

"You think one rotten tomato will stop me from my quest?" called Theseus. "No!"

"Let's see if fifty will do the trick!" shouted a Cretan, and tomatoes began flying through the air. Soon Theseus was dripping with tomato pulp. And, since most of the Cretans were lousy shots, so were the other XIII.

"Cut it out, Theseus!" hissed one of the XIII.

"Do!" said another. "Or the monster will think we're a tasty serving of mortals marinara!"

"You shall not die," Theseus told his cart mates. "For I shall save you!" Then he turned to the Cretan crowd once more. "My father is King Aegeus of Athens!" he shouted. "I swore to him that I would slay the Minotaur. And so I shall!"

"No way!" brayed the crowd.

"Yes way!" Theseus shouted back. "We shall sail safely back to Athens. I promised my father to change the ship's sails from black to white as a signal that I have killed the Minotaur!"

"Oh, cut the bull!" called a Cretan.

"Did I mention that I shall not do it the easy way?" called Theseus.

"Yes!" shouted the other XIII young Athenians. "You did!"

Theseus kept ranting to the crowd about how he was going to get the Minotaur. And the Cretans kept pelting him. At last, they ran out of tomatoes. But by that time, Theseus and the others were soaked to the skin.

The cart with the sauce-splattered victims rolled on. I stuck invisibly with it. At last we came to a large plaza. The cart stopped between a fountain containing a life-size statue of a bull and the royal palace. I'm a god. I'm not easy to impress. But when I saw the royal palace at Knossos, my godly mouth dropped open in awe. It was seven stories tall and had more columns than I could count. Staircases spiraled up the outside walls, connecting the floors to one another. The walls were covered in brightly painted murals of brawny bulls. The roof peaks were decorated with huge golden bulls' horns. Clearly the Cretans took their bulls very seriously.

I spotted a mortal wearing a big gold crown. Had to be King Minos. He was the absolute double of King di Minos, the judge and pizza chef, down in my kingdom. King Minos, Queen Pasiphae, and other royal types stood on the palace steps, watching as the Athens XIV were herded out of the cart. A little girl and a tall young woman with small gold crowns on their heads stood between the king and queen. They had to be the royal princesses.

"Move . . . back . . . from . . . the . . . roy . . . al . . . fam . . . i . . . ly!" Talos instructed the crowd. "No . . . push . . . ing! No . . . sho . . . ving."

Most quickly obeyed. A few stragglers were talking and didn't hear the instructions. When Talos noticed them, he reached into his bag, grabbed a stone, and hurled it in their direction.

Bonk!

"Ow!" cried a Cretan. He quickly moved back from the palace steps.

"Qui . . . et!" yelled Talos. The crowd grew still. Guards lined up the Athens XIV.

"Greetings, Athenians!" said King Minos. "Tomorrow you will be going in there." He pointed across the plaza to a huge gate. Stone letters curved over it that spelled L A B Y R I N T H.

"And," King Minos continued, "you won't come out."

Theseus shouted, "Yes, we will!"

The other XIII just whimpered.

But all the Cretans cheered.

"No one has ever escaped from the labyrinth," King Minos went on. King di Minos who lived down in my kingdom was a rat. But this relative of his was a thousand times worse! "It is full of passages that lead nowhere," Minos added. "That's why they're called *dead* ends."

Again, the Cretans cheered. They were a bloodthirsty bunch. I wondered why. And then I heard two Cretans talking.

"Thank Zeus for the Athens XIV," said one.

"Really," said the other. "If it weren't for them, King Minos would feed *us* to the Minotaur."

Well, that explained it.

"Oh, you can run," King Minos was telling the Athenian youths. "But you might run straight into the jaws of the Minotaur!"

"Ooooh!" squealed the crowd.

"Or you can hide," King Minos went on. "But at any moment, the terrible Minotaur could come round the corner and gobble you up!"

"Aaaaah!" cried the crowd. They really ate this up.

"There is no escape!" cried Minos.

Theseus hadn't shouted out anything else lately. I glanced over at the cart and saw why. Two of his fellow youths had their hands clapped over his mouth. They didn't want any more problems than they already had.

"Tomorrow," King Minos continued, "you will be led into the labyrinth. But tonight? We Cretans are going to throw you a great big all-night party!"

"Yay!" cried all the Cretans.

I glanced over at the Athens XIV. They looked suspicious. Especially Theseus. All this talk of doom. Now, suddenly, they were supposed to party?

"So live it up, Athenians!" cried King Minos. "Dance! Eat! Drink! Play games! Enjoy your last night of life!"

With that, a band started playing, and all the Cretans in the plaza started dancing.

Chapter XII

UN-BULL-IEVABLE!

The Athens XIV huddled together. They didn't seem to be in a party mood, marinated, as they were, in tomato sauce and scheduled for death-by-Minotaur the next day. Who could blame them?

I figured my best bet for helping Theseus would be to find the famous architect Daedalus. He'd built the labyrinth. Maybe I could get him to give me a map. I remembered Po saying that Daedalus lived in a penthouse on top of the palace. I could have taken the spiral staircases, but astro-traveling was quicker. *ZIP!* I found myself standing outside a door. A little brass plate said PENTHOUSE A, DAEDALUS AND ICARUS. I took off my helmet—*FOOP!*—I reappeared, and knocked.

All on its own, the door slowly swung open.

"Hello?" I called, stepping into the apartment. "Anybody home?"

Little bulbs embedded in the floor flickered on, making a path of light. I followed the path through a long hallway to a large, round room. It was empty. A thin, transparent tube attached to the walls circled the room. An alcove in the wall near where I stood held a small dish of clear glass marbles. It was an irresistible invitation. I picked up a marble and dropped it into the tube. The marble began traveling through the tube, and as it went, a chandelier made of bulls' horns dropped from the ceiling. A carpet with a bull-hoof-print pattern slid out from under a wall. Panels opened in the walls, and tables, chairs, and benches, all decorated with bulls' horns, swung into place. The marble traveled around the room, finally dropping back into the bowl. By that time, the room was completely furnished. For the second time that night, my jaw dropped in amazement. It was un-bull-ievable!

At that time, we gods had lots of high-tech equipment. But most mortals still got excited when they rubbed two sticks together and made a spark. Daedalus was clearly an exception.

Now a chair whirled around, and I found myself facing a mortal with a shock of white hair. He wore a bright blue robe and looked very pleased with himself.

"How do you like it?" he asked, not getting up.

"Very nice," I said. "You must be Daedalus."

"Bingo," said Daedalus. "And you must be Hades, Ruler of the Underworld."

I smiled. Finally, a mortal who got it right!

"Take a seat," said Daedalus, with a nod toward an oversize chair. "That one's god-size. I always hoped I'd have someone to fill it."

"Thanks," I said sitting down. "Very comfy."

Daedalus smiled. "This is a rare treat for me, King Hades. I don't get many visitors up here. The only one who comes regularly is the king's eldest daughter, Ariadne."

"Ariadne," I said. "About eighteen? Tall? Brown hair? Little crown?"

Daedalus nodded. "She likes my inventions. Very curious girl. Smart too. She's good friends with my delinquent son, Icarus, though I don't know how she puts up with him. He never does a thing I tell him. He never obeys me. Thirsty, Hades?"

"I wouldn't mind a glass of something."

As I finished speaking, a small self-propelled table scooted across the floor toward us. On it sat a jug and two goblets. Daedalus poured us each some wine.

"So, Daedalus, I understand you're the architect of the dreaded labyrinth," I said, taking a sip. Very smooth.

Daedalus nodded. "Designed every twist and turn."

"If you were led into the labyrinth, could you find your way out again?" I asked.

"Oh, no," said Daedalus. "Quite impossible. The thing is way too complicated."

"What are the chances of someone's being led into the labyrinth and accidentally stumbling back to the entrance?" I asked him.

"Exactly two-hundred billion to one."

Not good.

"But how did you and the workers get out when you were building it?" I asked him.

"Ah!" said Daedalus. "We had the clew. A magical ball of string. My invention, of course. Each morning I tied one end of the clew to the gate. Then I put the clew down and told it where I wanted to go, and gave it a little pat. It unwound through the maze, right to the spot I'd told it to go. Very clever, huh?" He smiled. "When I wanted to leave, I just picked the clew up and followed the string out of the labyrinth, winding it up as I went. Ingenious!"

"You think I could borrow the clew, Daedalus?" I asked. "One of the Athens XIV is my nephew, and I'd like to help him out."

Daedalus shook his white head. "Sorry, Hades. Can't do it. There's only one clew. It's the only way into the maze in case of an emergency. It's just too valuable to lend out."

"I understand," I told him.

"Icarus and Ariadne like to fool around with it sometimes," Daedalus said. "But I'm very strict about them keeping it inside the apartment. Wish I could help you out, Hades. Really do."

"Not a problem," I said. "I'll think of something." I stood up to go.

"Just follow the lights out, Hades," Daedalus said. "Come see me again."

"Will do," I said. Then I stopped. "By the way," I added, "did you make King Minos's robot security guard?"

"Not me." Daedalus shook his head. "No, I'd never make anything that nasty. Talos was a gift to Crete from Zeus."

Zeus! I should have known.

I thanked Daedalus for the wine and left Penthouse A. I walked about halfway down the spiral staircase. Then I stopped, pulled my phone out my pocket, and punched in some numbers.

"Cupid?" I said when he picked up. "It's Hades. Meet me on the palace steps in Knossos, Crete, on the double. I've got a job for you."

Chapter XIII

DEARLY BULL-LOVED

ZIP! Cupid landed on the palace steps in under five minutes. I was glad to see he'd brought his bow and arrows.

"I was right in the middle of dinner, man!" he said. "Psyche made lasagne. It's delicious! She's practicing Italian dishes for when my mom comes to visit. Whoa!" he said, finally noticing the big party scene in the plaza. "What's happening here?"

"It's a farewell party for some kids from Athens," I said, skipping all the gory details. I, too, surveyed the scene. I was glad to see that the Athens XIV had been allowed to shower and put on fresh robes. Most of them seemed to be trying to have a good time.

"So what's up, Hades?" asked Cupid. "I want to get back home and finish my dinner before it gets cold."

"We'll make it quick then. Come on." We ran down the steps and into the crowd. I didn't bother with my helmet. In this crowd, no one would notice a couple of random gods.

Mortals were dancing and eating all sorts of yummy-looking concoctions from food carts that surrounded the plaza. Others were playing carnival-type games like Throw a Hoop Around a Pillar. And Pop the Inflated Pig's Bladder. I spotted Theseus. He was in a group doing the limbo.

Two mortals held a long bar about two feet off the ground.

"That's too easy!" said Theseus. "Make it lower!"

That Theseus! He never changed.

The bar holders shook their heads, but lowered the bar.

Theseus bent back until his head almost touched

the ground. He began hopping toward the bar.

"That's Theseus, doing the limbo," I told Cupid. "Wait here. I'll get Ariadne. When she looks at Theseus, zing her with a three-day dose of love potion."

"Got it," said Cupid.

I found the princess dancing halfheartedly with a skinny young mortal. I tapped him on the shoulder and cut in.

"How would you like to dance with Theseus, one of the Athens XIV?" I asked Ariadne, as we started dancing. "It would mean the world to him, it being his last night and all."

"Is he a good dancer?" asked Ariadne. "That last guy danced like a codfish."

"Come over here," I said. "I'll show you which one he is, and you can decide."

Ariadne let me lead her over to the limbo dancers.

"Too easy!" Theseus was saying, even though the bar was only inches from the ground. "Lower!" Theseus leaned way back and started doing the little hops.

"Him? No way!" said Ariadne. "The limbo is the *worst*. These guys are freaks."

"You won't think so in a second," I muttered, giving Cupid the sign.

"What do you mean?" asled Ariadne.

"Look what Theseus is doing now," I said, and she did.

ZING!

"Ow!" Ariadne slapped at the back of her neck where a little golden arrow had pierced her skin. "It's buggy out to—" She stopped talking. She stared at Theseus. Then she skipped over to the limbo bar, which Theseus was somehow managing to squeeze under.

"Theseus, hi!" she said when he'd come out on the other side. "I'm Ariadne. That was amazing. I've always wanted to try the limbo. Think you could show me how?"

"Yes," said Theseus. "Watch me do it again. Pay particular attention to how I bend my knees. That's key."

"I'm done here," said Cupid.

"So you are. Nice shot, Cupid."

"Anything for you, man," Cupid said, giving me a little salute. "Lasagne time." Then—*ZIP!*—he was gone.

I put my helmet on—*POOF!*—and tailed Theseus. Ariadne was clearly head over heels in love with him. She stuck by his side all night. He didn't seem to mind.

At last dawn dawned. The band struck up "The Party's Over." And the drummer announced that this would be the last song. "Especially for you Athenians," he added.

Ariadne's face fell. She whispered to Theseus that she'd be right back. I followed her as she sprinted over to a young man. He looked like a black-haired version of Daedalus.

"Icarus," said Ariadne. "You have to help me out." She leaned over and whispered something in his ear.

Icarus broke into a sly grin. "Sure. Why not?" he said. "The old man will never miss it. Wait here. Be back in a flash."

And in a flash, he returned. He slipped something to Ariadne.

"Thanks, Icarus," she whispered. "Really."

I followed Ariadne as she hurried back to Theseus. I hated to spy on any tender moments, but I had to know whether my little scheme was going to work.

"Theseus, take this." Ariadne reached into the pocket of her robe and pulled out a tightly wound ball of bright orange string. She gave it to Theseus.

"What's this?" asked Theseus.

"It's the clew," said Ariadne. "It's to help you find your way back out of the labyrinth."

"No!" said Theseus, tossing the clew back to Ariadne as if it were a hot coal. "That would be the easy way!"

"But there is no other way," said Ariadne. "Trust me on this. If you go into the labyrinth without the clew, you'll never find your way back out. And . . . I'll never see you again."

"I am a hero," Theseus declared. "Heroes never do anything the easy way."

Ariadne rolled her eyes. "Couldn't you, just this once?"

"No," said Theseus. "Hercules is my role model. He would never take the clew."

"Hercules?" said Ariadne. "Of course he would! He'd take it in a minute!"

"You think?" said Theseus.

"Absolutely."

"Well, if you're sure." Theseus held out his hand and Ariadne gave him the clew.

"When you go into the labyrinth, have the other Athenians huddle around you while you tie the end of the clew to the gate," Ariadne told him. "Then put the clew on the ground, give it a little tap, and ask it to lead you to the Minotaur."

"And when I find him, I shall slay him!" declared Theseus.

"Don't go all the way to the Minotaur," said Ariadne. "Stop in one of the passageways and let the clew roll on. Wait there until nightfall. Then follow the clew back out of the labyrinth. No one has ever come out of the labyrinth. So no one will be watching. But I will be waiting for you."

Theseus frowned. "This is sounding very easy."

"It's not!" said Ariadne. "And, Theseus? When you are free again, will you take me back to Athens and marry me?"

"No!" said Theseus. "That would be too easy!"

"Easy?" said Ariadne. "It would be the opposite of easy!"

Ariadne was a quick study. I could see that she had Theseus all figured out.

"My father will be against such a marriage," Ariadne was saying. "He will send his army to do battle with you if you try to take me to Athens."

"He will?" Theseus smiled.

A roar sounded from inside the labyrinth. A second roar followed, accompanied by a terrible clatter.

"Athenians!" called a guard. "The Minotaur awaits you! Line up by height at the labyrinth gate. Shortest to tallest. That's the way it's done."

"Good luck, Theseus," Ariadne whispered. "I'll be waiting!" She gave him a kiss on the cheek, then ran off to stand with her family on the palace steps.

King Minos made a quick speech. He thanked the Athens XIV for the great sacrifice they were about to make. Then the Knossos Junior High School Marching Band began to play. The crowd cheered, and the Athens XIV marched through the gate. Theseus was the tallest, so he was the last to disappear into the labyrinth. With a loud clank, the guard swung the gate shut.

The crowd cheered one last time. Then their long night of dancing seemed to catch up with them, and they slowly headed home for a quick nap before the day began. The vendors closed their carts and rolled them off. Ariadne ran into the palace, presumably to pack.

Soon, I was the only one left on the plaza, and I was invisible. I spotted something lying beside the gate. What was it? I walked over to it. My godly heart nearly stopped when I saw what it was. The clew! Theseus had forgotten it.

Chapter XIV

RAWHIDE-AND-SEEK

Theseus had tied the clew to the labyrinth gate. But that's as far as he'd gotten.

I pushed on the gate. I was surprised when it swung open easily. But it made sense. Why lock it? No one wanted to go in. And no one could find the way out.

I gave the clew a little pat, and said, "Find Theseus!"

Just as Daedalus had said it would, the ball of string began rolling, unraveling as it went. I followed the clew through the labyrinth passageways, turning this way and that way, and this way again. No wonder no one could find their way out. This place was impossible!

I zigzagged after the clew for a long time, but I saw no sign of the Athens XIV. I imagined that Theseus was setting a swift pace through the labyrinth, even though he had to be hopelessly lost.

At long last, I heard a voice.

"Come on, Athenians!" It could only be Theseus. "The faster we go, the faster we'll find the Minotaur."

"But we don't *want* to find the Minotaur," one of the XIV said.

"You're the only one who wants to do that," said another.

"The rest of us just want to get out of here," said yet another.

I caught up with Theseus, and the clew stopped rolling. I picked it up.

Theseus saw me. "Hades!" he exclaimed. "What are you doing here?"

"Oh, just taking a little stroll." I held up the clew. "The other end of this ball of string is tied to the gate," I said. "All you have to do is turn around and follow it out of here."

"Yay!" cried the Athens XIII.

"No!" cried Theseus. "That would be too easy!"

The others groaned. I could tell they were thoroughly sick of Theseus and his high-and-mighty hero standards.

"Besides," said Theseus. "I have vowed to slay the Minotaur. And so I shall!"

If I could have talked him out of this crazy idea, I would have. But I knew better. All I could do was stick close and try to keep him from getting clobbered. I turned to the XIII. "The rest of you can go. Just follow the string."

"No!" Theseus cried again. He turned to face the XIII. "I thought we were all buddies together on this road trip."

Not the road trip again!

"We're not off on some adventure," said one of the XIII.

"No!" said another. "We were unlucky enough to be chosen by lottery to be fed to the Minotaur.

And now we're lucky enough to have a way out of here. I, for one, am taking it!"

"Yes, yes!" echoed the others.

"Okay, maybe this isn't a regular road trip," admitted Theseus. "But we've been through a lot together. The trip in the black-sailed ship. Being shoved into a cart."

"Being pelted with tomatoes," put in one of the XIII.

"Right!" exclaimed Theseus. "So we've bonded. We're buddies. Aren't we?"

No one answered him.

"Aren't we?" said Theseus.

"Mmm, well, yeah, sure," the others grudgingly admitted.

"Okay, then!" said Theseus. "Buddies don't desert each other." He turned to me. "We're sticking together, Hades. No one's leaving. We're going to find the Minotaur *together*."

More groaning from the XIII.

"All right," I said. "But let's at least follow the clew." I raised my hand to stop the objection I knew Theseus would raise. "I know, I know. It's the easy way. But we could wander around in here for *months.* Wouldn't you like to get to the Minotaur and get it over with?"

"I guess," said Theseus, although he clearly would have preferred to do it his way, no matter how long it took.

I dropped the clew again, tapped it with my toe, and said, "To the Minotaur!"

It began speeding away, and we all took off after it. Even Theseus. We turned so many times we got dizzy. After a while, we started bumping into each other. No one knew which direction we were going.

And then, just when I thought we might be bumbling through that labyrinth forever, we heard voices. Not roars. Not bellows. Mortal voices. We slowed down. Keeping together, we walked cautiously on. We turned a corner and there it was— the end of the maze! We started running and deka-seconds later we sprinted out onto a grassy plain. It was surrounded on all sides by high stone walls. My jaw nearly dropped open yet again. I had no idea where the labyrinth would end, but I wasn't expecting green grass and broad daylight.

As we all stood there, awestruck, a loud voice boomed out:

"Welcome!" it said. "You have reached the heart of the labyrinth."

Chapter XV

THE MINOTAUR

Who said that?

The Athens XIV huddled around me. For once, even Theseus had nothing to say. Where had the voice come from? I couldn't tell. But in the center of the field, I saw what looked like a wrestling ring. Around it, in smaller rings, some two dozen mortals, both men and women, were wrestling. Or practicing wrestling techniques. And they were good. The best wrestlers I'd ever seen. I pinched myself. Was I dreaming?

Now a tall, muscular mortal came toward us. He

looked like any other mortal, except that on top of his neck sat the head of a bull.

"Welcome!" he said. He smiled, showing his large, flat teeth. "So you got here, safe and sound."

"Are you the Minotaur?" asked Theseus.

"Technically, yes," said the bull-headed mortal. He was chewing a large wad of green stuff. "At least that's what I'm called when it suits people to think of me as a terrible flesh-eating monster."

"You mean you're *not* a terrible flesh-eating monster?" asked one of the XIV.

"Hardly." The Minotaur rolled his big brown eyes. "My name is Asterius," he said. "I'm a vegetarian. I've got horns, a furry face, and a big, wet, black nose. But other than that, I'm just like you. Well, one more thing. Excuse me for a moment." He turned his head and spat out a stream of green juice. "I also chew my cud," he added, wiping his mouth.

"Then how did all of Crete come to believe you are a monster?" asked Theseus.

"I'd be glad to tell you," said Asterius. "But you must be hungry after your long hike through the labyrinth.

Come! Let's eat lunch while I tell you my story."

I liked Asterius instantly. We followed him over to a shady area where several picnic tables had been set up for lunch. We sat down and servants brought out platters of whole-grain breads and a big selection of wild grasses, lettuces, and leaves. Luckily, I still had my Ambrosia Power Bar. When I finished that, I sprinkled Ambro-Salt on the bread and lettuce, and settled down to an extremely high-fiber, godly meal.

"I was only eight when I came to live in the labyrinth," Asterius began, helping himself to a large portion of grass. "For a year or so, I was happy here with my tutors and Xenon, my wrestling coach."

"So you've been a wrestler for a long time," I said, wondering if he might be UWF material.

Asterius nodded. "But I wanted other kids around to wrestle with, so I started bellowing and banging around. At the time, my dad was angry with King Aegeus. He wanted to punish Athens, so he came up with the idea of saying he'd sack the city unless King Aegeus sent seven young men and seven maidens to be fed to the Minotaur."

"But really they were sent to be your wrestling partners?" asked Theseus.

"Exactly," said Asterius. "Dad came up with the whole bit about the black-sailed ship and the all-night farewell party." The Minotaur shrugged. "His subjects really eat that stuff up. So anyway, when the first kids got here, Xenon set up a little wrestling school. We had a great time. You should have seen our tag-team matches! But after a while, we got to know each other's moves as well as we knew our own. We got sick of wrestling each other."

"That's where the every nine years comes in," guessed one of the latest XIV.

"Yes, we need new opponents every now and then," Asterius said. "So we all roar and make as much racket as we can, and pretty soon another shipload of Athenians shows up."

Asterius took his napkin and blotted some grass juice from his furry chin.

Theseus stood up. "Wrestle me, Asterius!"

Asterius grinned. "All right," he said. "But let's wait an hour or so until we've digested our fodder. I mean, our lunch."

"All right," said Theseus. "And since you've been so open with us," he added, "I feel it is my duty to tell you that I have vowed to slay you."

"Oh, come on, Theseus!" cried the XIII.

But, Asterius held up a hand for silence. "I understand," he said. "You thought I was a horrible flesh-eating monster. You thought slaying me would be a heroic deed."

"Right," said Theseus.

"But now you've met me," Asterius went on. "Now you see that I'm not a monster. I can get a little rough in the ring, but outside of it, I wouldn't hurt a flea."

Theseus frowned. "I can see that," he said. "But a vow is a vow. We heroes take our vows seriously. I have vowed to slay you, and so I must."

"But, Theseus," said one of the XIII. "You didn't have all the facts!"

"Can't a hero change his mind?" asked another.

Theseus shook his head. "Not when it comes to a vow."

I had to step in. "Theseus, you forget practically

everything," I reminded him. "Couldn't you forget this one little vow?"

"No way," said Theseus.

"How do you plan to slay me, Theseus?" Asterius asked. "With a sword?"

"No!" said Theseus. "That would be too easy."

"With a club?" asked Asterius.

"No!" said Theseus. "Easy!"

"Well, how then?" asked Asterius.

"With my bare hands," said Theseus.

"Ah!" said Asterius eagerly. "You're talking wrestling!"

"What else?" said Theseus.

"So we shall go at it until one of us slays the other?" asked Asterius.

"Right," said Theseus. "And I'll win!"

Asterius stood up. "Everyone!" he shouted. "Come to the center ring! Theseus and I are going to wrestle each other to the death!"

Chapter XVI

GORE-Y

All the wrestling mortals stopped what they were doing and ran toward the big center ring. Asterius and Theseus jumped up onto the raised platform, ducked under the ropes, and went to opposite corners.

An older mortal wearing a robe with XENON on the pocket went over to Asterius. He began helping him limber up.

"Hades!" called Theseus. "Come be my coach!"

How could I say no? I hopped into the ring.

"All right, Theseus," I said. "You've got a few

inches and a few pounds on Asterius. I think you can take him. But no head-locks. If you get gored by those horns, things could get messy."

Theseus nodded.

Asterius walked to the center of the ring. "Come and get me if you can, Theseus!" he taunted him.

Theseus flew out of his corner like an arrow shot from Cupid's bow. The two wrestlers wasted no time in showing off their flying kicks and ankle-locks. Asterius tried a tummy butt, but Theseus wisely jumped out of the way. I'd never seen such great wrestling. Amazing! It was better than any match I'd seen in Wrestle Dome in Thebes. Even Cyclops, my favorite Wrestling Immortal, would have had a hard time pinning either of these guys to the mat.

The labyrinth wrestlers cheered for Asterius.

"Go, Bully!" they called to him. "Butt him out of the ring!"

The Athens XIII loyally cheered for Theseus.

"Stop that bull, Theseus!" cried one.

"Get him, buddy!" cried another.

On and on they wrestled. Finally, Theseus's eyes took on a half-dazed look. Asterius's big brown bull eyes didn't have that much expression, so it was hard to tell how he was feeling. But he was sweating up a storm. They both moved in slow motion. They both looked as if they might drop dead from exhaustion. This wasn't wrestling anymore. They'd had enough.

"It's a tie!" I cried.

"No!" cried all the mortals. "Boo! Boo!"

Theseus tried to object, but he was too woozy to speak.

Everyone booed me. But I stood in the center of the ring with my arms folded across my chest, and held firm. Hanging out with ghosts, I was used to booing. I waited for it to die down. When it finally did, I spoke to the crowd.

"Theseus and Asterius are the world's best wrestlers," I said. "You've just seen an historic match. Let's face it. Both these guys are winners!"

There was a smattering of applause.

"And I know they'll wrestle again," I went on. "May the best man or Minotaur win!"

Now the mortals cheered for real.

"I wish all of you here long, full mortal lives," I continued, nodding toward the spectators. "But since you are mortal, one day you're all going to end up as ghosts in my kingdom."

Everyone stared blankly at me. Including Asterius and Theseus.

"So, since you'll all be down there together," I wound up, "maybe you'd like to see these guys have a rematch in the Underworld Wrestling Federation."

The crowd went wild, cheering and whistling and shouting, "Rematch! Rematch!"

As the cheering went on, I whipped out two more UWF contracts. In the excitement of the moment, both Asterius and Theseus signed on the dotted line. Yes!

The spectators wandered off then. Theseus and Asterius headed for the showers. I rested on the grass, imagining how the UWF would soon become an awesome force in the wrestling cosmos!

In a while, Asterius came over to me. He was showered and smelling as sweet as possible for a bull. He sat down beside me.

"Hades," he said, "did you see the twenty-eight labyrinth wrestlers in action today?"

"I did," I told him.

"Are they any good?" asked Asterius. "I mean compared to what's going on out in the world?"

"Every one of them could be a champ at Wrestle Dome in Thebes," I told him. "In the MD—Mortals Division—of course. They'd really give the sport a huge lift."

Asterius broke into another bullish grin. "That's what I was hoping to hear. Even though no one's said so, I can tell that they'd all like a chance to live out in the world again. And I wondered if they were good enough to make a living as pros."

"Definitely," I said, growing excited about this idea. "I'd be happy to take them up to Wrestle Dome myself. Make sure they meet the right mortals. But how about you, Asterius? You could definitely be MD world champ. Aren't you ready to see what life is like outside this maze?"

Asterius shrugged. "I don't know," he said. "I'm past thirty now. That's old for a wrestler. And in here, I forget that I have a bull's head. Everyone treats me as if I'm normal. Pardon me," he said politely. He turned his head to the side and spat out a slimy green wad. "But out in the world?" He shook his bull head. "It would be a different story."

"I know some Naiads with dog heads," I told Asterius. "And my good friends, the Furies, have live snakes instead of hair. But come to think of it, they're not mortals. I guess that makes a big difference. We immortals have lived so long and seen so much that nothing really throws us for a loop."

"I'm happy here, Hades," Asterius said. "I've got all the grass I can eat, Xenon's a great coach, and I have plenty of wrestling buddies. Don't worry about me." He jumped up. "I'll tell the others about your offer, though. They can decide. Thanks, Hades!" And he ran off.

That night at dinner, Asterius stood up. He told all the wrestlers how I'd offered to introduce them into the world of pro wrestling. "Anyone who wants to stay can stay," he said. "But if you're ready to go, that's cool."

He asked for a show of hands. Twenty of the twenty-eight labyrinth wrestlers voted to leave. But thirteen of the latest fourteen—all but Theseus—voted to stay. They understood that they'd get excellent coaching from Xenon, and when they left, they could have hot wrestling careers themselves.

"I shall go," said Theseus. "I am a hero, and there are bullies I must wrestle and monsters I must slay. Real ones," he added.

We bedded down out in the field that night, looking up at the stars. The next morning, we said good-bye to Asterius and the Athens XIII. Then, with the twenty labyrinth wrestlers, I followed Theseus as he wound the string of the clew back into a ball. The string was slippery and hard to wind, so Theseus didn't object that it was too easy. By evening, we reached the gate.

I peered out into the plaza. Throngs of Cretans were strolling in all directions. Good.

"Meet me at the harbor in an hour," I told the wrestlers. Then, one by one, they slipped out onto the plaza. They were quickly swept up in the crowd, and Talos never spotted them.

As I watched the wrestlers go, I noticed a small figure sitting next to a large backpack on the palace steps. Theseus and I were the last to leave the labyrinth. The figure on the steps jumped up and ran toward us. It was Ariadne.

"Theseus?" she called. "Is that you?"

Obviously Cupid's potion was still going strong.

"Shhh!" Theseus put his finger to his lips.

Ariadne nodded and began hurrying along beside us. "I've bribed the captain of the black-sailed ship," she whispered. "He's waiting for us. He's promised to sail us back to Greece where we can be married!"

"No!" said Theseus.

"You . . . you mean you don't want to marry me?" Ariadne stopped. She looked crushed.

"No!" said Theseus. "I mean I won't sail on a ship where the captain has been bribed. That would be too easy!"

"Oh, no, it won't!" said Ariadne. "Talos, the robot, is sure to spot us running for the ship. He will hurl rocks at us."

"He will?" said Theseus.

"Yes," said Ariadne. "And if that doesn't stop us, he will cause himself to burst into flames. Then he'll chase us and try to set us on fire!"

"He will?" said Theseus.

"Yes," said Ariadne. "And if that doesn't stop us,

Talos will hurl huge stones at the black-sailed ship and try to sink it."

"He will?" said Theseus.

"Yes," said Ariadne. "And if that doesn't stop us, he'll order out my father's fleet of one-hundred ships to set sail and chase us. My father's sailors will shoot at us with flaming arrows!"

"They will?" said Theseus.

"Yes!" said Ariadne.

"Well, what are we waiting for?" cried Theseus. He grabbed Ariadne's hand and started to run. "To the ship!"

Chapter XVII

HORRI-BULL TRIP

Theseus couldn't wait to do battle with Talos. Me? I wasn't all that excited about being chased, pelted with rocks, set on fire, or shot at with flaming arrows. So I did the sensible thing and put on my helmet. *POOF!*

Invisible, I ran beside Ariadne and Theseus toward the harbor. As I went, the wind picked up. A storm was blowing in.

When we reached the harbor, I spotted the labyrinth wrestlers. They were on the pier, cowering behind Old Plato's Bait Shack, trying to hide from the giant robot.

But Talos was on to them.

"Come . . . out . . . stran . . . gers!" the robot called. "O . . . bey! Or . . . Ta . . . los . . . will . . . be . . . forced . . . to . . . throw . . . rocks . . . at . . . you! Big . . . ones!"

The twenty stayed put.

Talos began pelting the bait shack with rocks.

"Hey!" Old Plato yelled out the little window. "Cut that out!"

But Talos kept pelting.

The twenty wrestlers hunkered down.

"O . . . kay!" called Talos. "Ta . . . los . . . warned . . . you!"

With that, the robot stomped over to the bait shack. When he got close to it, he closed his metal eyes, clenched his metal fists, and burst into flames. The old boards of the shack instantly caught fire. Old Plato ran out just as the thing went up in smoke, wailing, "My bait! My bait!"

"Follow me!" Theseus called to the wrestlers. "The smoke will give us cover!"

He ran down the dock past the smoking shack toward a fleet of rowboats at the end of the pier.

The wrestlers ran through the smoke after him. I followed invisibly behind. Talos, still burning, charged after us. When I reached the end of the dock, I looked over my shoulder. The flaming robot was still coming. But the fire at the bait shop had been put out. In fact, Plato was nailing a sign to the charred remains of the shack. It said OLD PLATO'S FRIED CLAMS.

Theseus and Ariadne were the first to reach the rowboats. They jumped into one, and Theseus started rowing. The twenty wrestlers jumped into other rowboats. They began rowing over the choppy water toward the black-sailed ship. The sky was very dark and the wind was high. Raindrops began to fall.

"Stop!" Talos shouted. "In . . . the . . . name . . . of . . . King . . . Min . . . os!"

The robot kept shouting as he clomped toward the rowboats. When he reached the end of the pier, he stepped right off it into the harbor. A great cloud of steam rose and he sizzled loudly as his fire went out. He kept walking. He was so tall that the water came only to his waist. Without missing a step, he waded forward, throwing rocks at the rowboats as he went.

Clunk!

Talos scored a hit. One of the rowboats sprang a leak. It started going down.

"Help!" cried the wrestlers. "We can't swim!"

Talos sloshed through the water, grinning his metal grin and gaining on them.

There was only one thing to do. *ZIP!* I astro-traveled to that rowboat.

"Yikes!" cried the wrestler at the oars as I landed invisibly in his lap.

I took off my helmet. *FOOP!*

"Move over, mortal!" I grabbed the oars. I motioned to another wrestler. "You, plug the leak. The rest of you? Bail!" Then I began rowing with all my godly might through the driving rain toward the black-sailed ship.

Talos was still pelting us. I zigzagged through the harbor, dodging the rocks.

Theseus and Ariadne's rowboat was the first to reach the ship. They hopped aboard. They held their hands out to help the wrestlers get on. I jumped aboard, too.

Now Talos began calling out the Cretan ships:

"Roy . . . al . . . na . . . vy! Red . . . a . . . lert!"

The crews of the one hundred ships in the harbor ran onto the decks.

"Ship . . . cap . . . tains!" Talos's metal voice boomed out across the harbor. "Pur . . . sue . . . the . . . black . . . sailed . . . ship!"

The captains began shouting orders.

The captain of the black-sailed vessel began barking orders to his crew, too. The sailors at the oars began to row us out of the harbor. Theseus grabbed an oar and rowed, too.

Minos's one hundred ships rowed out of the harbor after us.

"See, Theseus?" Ariadne called to him. "What did I tell you?"

Once out in the open sea, our crew hoisted the black sails. The wind caught them. We began racing over the choppy water.

King Minos's ships raised their sails, too. They sped after us. Now they began firing flaming arrows.

THUNK!

"We're hit!" yelled a wrestler as an arrow found its mark in the side of the ship. Small flames spurted up. Flaming arrows began to fly now, thick and fast. But thanks to the pouring rain, their fires quickly went out.

Fewer and fewer arrows hit us, and finally they stopped.

"We've outrun Minos's fleet!" cried the first mate.

Everyone cheered!

In all the excitement, I hadn't noticed the high waves. Or the wind, rocking the ship wildly with every gust. It wasn't until the cheering died down that it hit me—I was seasick!

I ran to the side of the ship.

Ariadne was already there. "Ohhhh," she groaned. "I feel awful."

"Me, too," I said.

"How long till we get to Athens?" she asked.

"Three, four days," I managed.

"Ohhhhh," groaned Ariadne. "I'll never live that long."

Even though I was immortal, I knew just how she felt. I was very tempted to astro-travel to Athens. But I couldn't desert Ariadne when she was feeling so sick. After all, it was all my fault that she'd fallen for Theseus and had ended up on this ship.

"Let me see what I can do." I fumbled in my robe pocket and pulled out my phone. I hit memory dial for Po, god of the seas. Maybe I could get him to stop this storm.

"Yo! You've reached Po!"

Oh, no! I'd gotten his voice mail.

"Hear the beep and talk to me, baby. I'll call ya back. In the meantime, party on!" *BEEP!*

"Po? Hades. On ship. Near Crete. Terrible storm. Sick as a dog. Stop storm, Po. Hurry!" I hung up. I didn't hold out much hope that Po would come to our rescue.

Ariadne turned her head toward me slightly. "Is he going to stop the storm?"

"If he gets the message."

"Ohhhhh," groaned Ariadne. "I hope he does!"

Just then the captain of the ship came by. He saw us hanging miserably over the rail.

"Ah, feeling seasick?" he said briskly. "Don't worry. In a day or two, it'll pass. Then you'll get your appetite back. And I'll invite you to join me at the captain's table for steamed lobster with melted butter and shrimp and mussels and scallops and—Eeech! You really *are* sick!"

By the time Ariadne lifted her head, the captain was gone. But Theseus was at her side.

"Ariadne," he said. "You look . . . awful!"

"Thanks," she managed. "Do you see that island over there, Theseus?" She pointed.

Theseus squinted through the driving rain. "I see it," he said.

"We must stop there," said Ariadne. "It's a matter of life or death. Tell the captain, will you. Theseus?"

"No!" said Theseus. "Stopping there would be too easy."

"Theseus," I said. "Come over here." It took all my energy, in my seasick state, but I pulled him aside. "We're all on this trip together. We're all buddies, aren't we?"

Theseus smiled. "Right!"

"And buddies help each other out," I said. "Ariadne and I need to get off this ship until the storm passes. It's not about what's too easy. It's about buddies helping buddies."

Now Theseus got it.

"No problem, Hades," he said. "I'll go tell the captain."

And in less than an hour, the ship pulled close to the deserted island of Naxos. One of the crew rowed Ariadne and me ashore. We staggered up onto the beach. We made it as far as the high tide line before we collapsed.

"Land," murmured Ariadne. She kissed the sand and fell instantly asleep.

My head was spinning. My stomach was churning. But how good to be on land. I, too, closed my eyes.

The next thing I knew, Ariadne was shaking me. "Hades! Hades!" she cried. "Wake up!"

"Huh?" I sat up. "What's wrong? Has your father's fleet come after us?"

"Worse!" said Ariadne. "Look!" She pointed out to sea. I could barely make out the tiny shape of the black-sailed ship. "The ship has left us here, Hades!" cried Ariadne. "Theseus is gone!"

Chapter XVIII

UNFORGETTA-BULL

"Don't take it personally," I told Ariadne. "Theseus just forgot."

"Forgot?" she said. "*Forgot?* No offense, Hades, but if Theseus forgot you, I could understand it. But how could he forget *me?*"

"He's very forgetful," I told her. "Really. It's not you. It's him."

"That is such a guy excuse," Ariadne muttered. She began pacing furiously up and down on the sand. "After all I did to help him, he just forgets me? Hey, what's that?" She put a hand to her brow to shade her eyes and looked out to sea. "Maybe Theseus is coming back!"

But it wasn't Theseus's ship that anchored off at Naxos. It was a crazy-looking craft made from the slats of wine barrels and loaded with overflowing picnic hampers. It belonged to Dionysus, the god of wine. Ariadne and I watched as several satyrs, wild nature gods with goat's horns and shaggy-haired goat's legs, rowed Dionysus ashore.

Dionysus spotted us standing on the beach. When his rowboat was near enough, he hopped out and waded ashore. He strode over to us.

"Hades," he said. "Nice surprise to see you." He turned toward Ariadne. "And who might you be, lovely creature?"

"I'm Ariadne," she said, "daughter of Queen Pasiphae and King Minos of Crete."

Dionysus picked up the hem of his robe, and with it, wiped a tear from Ariadne's cheek. "Why so sad, Ariadne?"

"Oh," said Ariadne, smiling up at the god, "I forget!"

Ariadne's smile told me that Cupid's three-day

dose had worn off. She was now walking down the beach holding hands with Dionysus. The satyrs had brought several picnic hampers ashore. Now they spread a tablecloth on the beach and set places for two. I had a feeling I wasn't needed anymore.

"Hey, Ariadne!" I called. "I think I'll be going now."

Ariadne turned and gave me a little wave. "Bye, Hades. Take care!"

ZIP! I astro-traveled straight to Athens. I wanted to meet Theseus and the other wrestlers as soon as they docked. I wanted to take them to Wrestle Dome personally and get them started on their hot wrestling careers. But first, I wanted to tell King Aegeus the good news—his son had not been devoured by the Minotaur. He was coming home.

I landed at King Aegeus's palace, on top of a high limestone cliff.

"Zeus's pajamas!" the ancient king cried, startled by my landing. "Are you some hooligan come to murder me? Don't bother! I'm not long for this world anyhow."

"It's Hades," I told the old king. "I came to tell you that—"

"Hold it." The old king held up a hand. "I'm getting darned tired of sitting on this stone throne, waiting to catch sight of my son's ship. How about getting me a cushion?"

"Be happy to," I told him. "But first, let me tell you some good news."

"It'll keep until you get the cushion," said the old king. "My poor bony backside. I've got no padding anymore."

I ducked into the palace. Whoa, it was a wreck. Since his wife had taken off in a cloud of green smoke, the place must have gone downhill. Several servants were snoozing on the couch. Clearly they thought the old king wouldn't notice if they slacked off.

I'd just found a little pillow and was taking it to the king, when I heard the king shouting something about the Minotaur!

I ran to the king.

But all I found was a servant standing beside the throne, shrieking.

"What's wrong?" I asked him. "Where's the king?"

The servant stopped shrieking. But he was too stunned to speak. He only pointed to the sea far below. I looked, but, all I could see was the sea. Then, on the horizon, I spied a ship. A ship with black sails. And I knew what had happened.

"Did the king jump up when he saw the ship?" I asked the servant.

The servant nodded.

"Did he yell that the Minotaur had eaten his son?" I asked.

Again, the servant nodded.

"And did he then leap into the sea?" I asked.

The servant shook his head.

"Didn't leap, huh?" I thought for a moment. "Did he clutch his chest, go limp, and fall into the sea?"

Now the servant nodded and scurried away.

So, after all these years, the sibyl's prophecy had come true. Long ago, King Aegeus had opened his wineskin in Troezen, far from the highest point in Athens. And now, when he had seen the black-sailed ship returning, he thought the Minotaur had eaten Theseus and so he had died of grief and toppled into the sea.

I stuck around the palace, rousing the servants and getting them to straighten up for all the Athenians I knew would be arriving soon. So I never did make it to the harbor to meet the black-sailed ship. And I didn't get to be the one to take the labyrinth wrestlers to Thebes and the Wrestle Dome. No, I waited at Aegeus's palace; and a few hours later, Theseus arrived. I broke the news to him about King Aegeus.

"Oops!" said Theseus. "Do you think it was because I forgot to change the sails?"

"There's a good chance," I said. "But he was very old, Theseus. He didn't have much time left."

Theseus frowned. "Dad will come down to your kingdom now, right Hades? Can you tell him I'm sorry?"

"Be glad to," I told him. "So, Theseus, you'll be crowned king of Athens now."

"Um, probably." Theseus didn't seem at all excited about becoming king. "And listen, Hades," he went on, "tell dad that my first act as king will be to rename this sea, the Blue Sea That My Dad Plunged into After He Died of Grief."

I frowned. "A bit on the long side, isn't it?" I said. "Why not honor your father's name? Call it something like—the Aegean Sea?"

"Hey, I like that." Theseus smiled. "Well, I have to go see somebody about some matter of ruling the city." He shrugged. "I hope you'll come to my coronation, Hades."

"I'd love to," I told him. "When is it?"

"Um . . ." Theseus shrugged again. "Ask around. I'm sure somebody will know."

"Will do." I made a mental note to call Po. I had a feeling he'd like to see his son crowned king. "By the way, Theseus," I added. "You don't have to worry about Ariadne."

"Ariadne!" exclaimed Theseus. "Oh my gosh, I totally forgot about her! Is she all right?"

"She's fine," I said. "I think she and Dionysus are getting married."

"She's marrying a god?" said Theseus. "I guess I missed my chance with her. Do you happen to know if she has any younger sisters?"

"One, I think," I told him.

Theseus and I walked out of the palace together.

"Theseus," I said as we went, "you know, there are classes you could take to improve your memory. Have you ever thought of signing up for one?"

"No!" said Theseus.

And this time, I said it with him: "That would be too easy!"

Epilogue

Now you know the truth about Theseus and the Minotaur. Now you can forget all about Zeus's bull-hooey version of the myth.

When I finished writing this book, I wanted to give the manuscript to my publisher, Hyperion, right away. But I was a little nervous. When I showed the old Titan my last book, he asked me to make all sorts of revisions. So this time I asked my first lieutenant, Hypnos, the god of sleep, to read it first. It took him a couple of weeks, but finally he came into the den one night, holding the manuscript.

He tossed it onto the coffee table and put his

hands on his hips. "You made it sound as if all I do is sleep on the job," he said.

Oops! I'd forgotten I'd put that into the story. I was getting as forgetful as Theseus.

I apologized to Hypnos and took the manuscript back from him. I read it myself, then. I hadn't read it since I'd finished writing it. Enough time had passed so that this time through, I caught things I hadn't noticed before, when I was in the fever of writing. I fixed things up, shifted things around, and when I was happy with the story, I had one of my ghosts deliver it to Hyperion.

The old Titan had given me tight deadlines. So the very next day, I began thinking about which myth to debunk next. I picked up *The Big Fat Book of Greek Myths* and went to sit beside the Pool of Memory, which seemed a fitting place to go after spending time writing about Theseus. I'd only been reading for an hour or so when I heard the sound of hoofbeats. I looked up. There was Hyperion, speeding down the pathway toward me in his rusty old chariot. He reined in his steeds, and hopped out.

"Hades, you lazy lout," he said, by way of a greeting. "Don't I pay you enough to write these stories?"

"You pay me plenty," I said.

"Then how come you stopped right in the middle of this one, boy? You left off with Theseus about to become king. He was still only sixteen! Surely there's more to the story."

"There's lots more," I said. "Theseus was a forgetful mortal, but one thing he never forgot was how to have a great adventure. He had tons of them."

"So how come you left out all the rest?" asked Hyperion.

"If I'd put all of Theseus's adventures into one book, it would be so heavy, it would take Hercules to lift it," I told him.

"Mortals love big thick heavy books, Hades," said Hyperion. "Don't you know that? Look what happened with those books about Harry What's-his-name. Sold like hotcakes."

The old Titan sat down next to me on the bench with my manuscript in his lap. "So tell me, Hades. Was Theseus a good king?"

"No," I said. "He kept longing for adventures and forgetting to rule."

"Dawg! I hate when kings do that."

"Theseus knew he was a lousy king," I went on. "So he went to Delphi and asked the sibyl what he should do."

"What did the sibyl say?" asked Hyperion.

"She told Theseus to give Athens a constitution. If he did that, she predicted that forever after, the Athenians would ride the stormy seas as safely as if they were riding on a pig's bladder."

"That is one strange prophecy, Hades," said Hyperion.

"It is," I agreed. "Theseus didn't even know what a constitution was. But his mom knew, from doing crossword puzzles. She told him it was a document that created rule by the people. So Theseus wrote out a constitution and made Athens the world's first democracy."

"What about that pig's bladder part?" asked Hyperion.

"Well, the closest I can come is that a pig's bladder full of air never sinks. And, in time, Athens became the shipping capital of the world. Ships from Athens sailed the seven seas and hardly ever sank."

"Dawg! That sibyl knows what she's talking about."

"She's often right, if you can figure out what she means," I told Hyperion.

"And what happened to Ariadne?" asked Hyperion. "I liked her spunk."

"She and Dionysus got married," I told him. "None of this Speedy Wedding Chapel stuff for them, either. They had a big wedding. Ariadne was mortal, of course. So in time, she came down to my kingdom. Dionysus took the diamond crown he had given her when they married and put it up in the sky, where it still shines among the stars."

"Whoo-whee," said Hyperion. "That is romantic."

"Theseus got married, too," I said.

"Who did he marry, Hades?" asked Hyperion.

"Ariadne's little sister, Phaedra," I said.

"No kidding!" said Hyperion. He grinned. "So Hades, you think we should ask the sibyl which myth you should write next?"

"No," I told him. "I think I've found a good one.

It's about Pandora." I picked up *The Big Fat Book of Greek Myths*. Here's the page I opened it to. Go on, read what it says:

The first mortal woman was a marble statue that was brought to life. Zeus named her Pandora. He gave her a box and told her not to open it, but she did. Out flew all sorts of evils— disease, pain, greed—that are still on earth to this day.

"Whoa!" said Hyperion. "Don't you wish she'd never opened that box, Hades?"

"She didn't really," I told him. "Zeus made that up. He wanted her to open the box because he'd bet me a bundle that she would. He tried everything, but he could never get her to do it. Finally it drove old

Zeus so crazy that he resorted to his lowest trick ever to get it opened."

"So all the evils in the world are his fault?" asked Hyperion.

"You could say that," I told him. "I'm thinking of calling the new book *Keep a Lid on It, Pandora!*"

"Sounds good to me," said Hyperion. "And listen, I don't want to pressure you or anything, but how about putting a couple of us Titans into this story? We big guys are starting to feel left out."

"Not a problem," I said.

"Thanks, buddy," said Hyperion. "One more question. Did you ever get the Underworld Wrestling Federation going?"

I smiled. "Drop by the stadium tonight and see for yourself," I told him. "It's Sinis 'The Pine Bender' going up against 'Mr. Nighty-Night' Procrustes. It's going to be a dynamite match!"

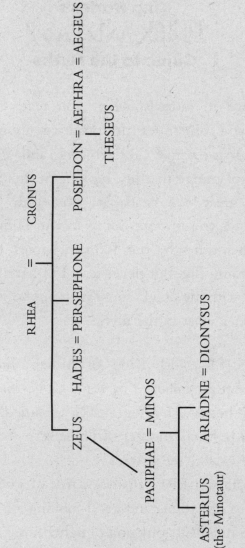

King Hades's
QUICK-AND-EASY
Family Tree of the Gods

RHEA = CRONUS

ZEUS   HADES = PERSEPHONE   POSEIDON = AETHRA = AEGEUS

THESEUS

PASIPHAE = MINOS

ASTERIUS   ARIADNE = DIONYSUS
(the Minotaur)

King Hades's
QUICK-AND-EASY
Guide to the Myths

Let's face it, mortals, when you read the Greek myths, you sometimes run into long, unpronounceable names—names like *Ariadne* and *Daedalus*—names so strange that just looking at them can give you a great big headache. Not only that, but sometimes you mortals call us by our Greek names, and other times by our Roman names. It can get pretty confusing. But never fear! I'm here to set you straight with my quick-and-easy guide to who's who and what's what in the myths.

Aegeus [EE-je-us]: King of Athens; husband of Aethra; believed by some to be the father of Theseus. The Aegean Sea is named for him.

Aethra [E-thra]: mother of Theseus.

Alec [AL-eck]: see **Furies**.

ambrosia [am-BRO-zha]: food that we gods must eat to stay young and good-looking for eternity.

Apollo [uh-POL-oh]: god of light, music, medicine,

poetry, and the sun; one of the Twelve Power Olympians; son of Zeus and Leto. The Romans call him Apollo, too.

Ariadne [air-ee-ADD-knee]: daughter of King Minos and Queen Pasiphae, who gave Theseus the clew to help him find his way out of the labyrinth.

Asphodel [AS-fo-del] **Fields**: the large region of the Underworld, home to the ghosts of those who were not so good, but not so bad on earth.

Athens [ATH-enz]: city of Athena, important city in ancient Greece.

Calydonian Boar [kal-uh-DOHN-ee-un]: a monstrous fire-breathing wild boar said to run a fine wrestling academy.

Cerberus [SIR-buh-rus]: my fine, three-headed pooch, guard dog of the Underworld.

Charon [CARE-un]: water taxi driver; ferries the living and the dead across the River Styx.

Crete [KREET]: an island in the Mediterranean Sea off the southern coast of Greece.

Cupid [KYOO-pid]: what the Romans called the

little god of love; we Greeks prefer **Eros**.

Cyclopes [SIGH-klo-peez]: three of many one-eyed giants, Lightninger, Shiner, and Thunderer, children of Gaia and Uranus, and uncles to us gods.

Daedalus [DEAD-uh-lus]: artist, inventor, builder of the labyrinth.

Delphi [DELL-fi]: an oracle in Greece on the southern slope of Mount Parnassus where a sibyl is said to predict the future.

Dionysus [die-uh-NI-sus]: son of Zeus and a mortal princess, Semele; god of wine. The Romans call him **Bacchus**.

Drosis [DRO-sis]: short for **theoexidrosis** [thee-oh-ex-uh-DRO-sis]: old Greek-speak for "violent god sweat."

Furies [FYOOR-eez]: three winged, serpent-haired immortals who pursue and punish wrongdoers, especially children who insult their mothers; their full names are Tisiphone, Megaera, and Alecto, but around my palace, they're known as Tisi, Meg, and Alec.

Gaia [GUY-uh]: Mother Earth, the beginning of all

life; married to Uranus, Father Sky; gave birth to the Titans, the Cyclopes, and the Hundred-Handed Ones; she's my Granny Gaia; don't upset her, unless you're up for an earthquake.

Hades [HEY-deez]: K.H.R.O.T.U.—King Hades, Ruler of the Underworld, that's me. I'm also God of Wealth, owner of all the gold, silver, and precious jewels in the earth. The Romans call me **Pluto**.

Hercules [HER-kew-leez]: son of Zeus; a major muscle-bound hero; won immortality by performing twelve labors concocted by Hera.

Hyperion [hi-PEER-ee-un]: a way cool Titan dude, once in charge of all light in the universe. Now owns a cattle ranch in the Underworld. Has a taste for good books.

Hypnos [HIP-nos]: god of sleep.

Icarus [ICK-ur-us]: son of Daedalus.

ichor [EYE-ker]: god blood.

immortal [ih-MORT-ul]: a being, such as a god or possibly a monster, who will never die—like me.

Knossos [NAW-soss]: a city of ancient Crete, the center of Minoan civilization.

Labyrinth [LAB-uh-rinth]: a complicated maze of interconnected passages in which the Minotaur was imprisoned.

Medea [mi–DEE–uh]: a princess and sorceress.

Meg [MEG]: see **Furies**.

Minos [MEE-noss]: ruler of Crete; extremely closely related to King di Minos, dweller in the Underworld.

Minotaur [MIN–uh–tor], named **Asterius** [as-TEAR-ee-us]: half man, half bull; once thought to have been slain by Theseus.

mortal [MORT-ul]: a being who one day must die; I hate to be the one to break this to you, but *you* are a mortal.

Mount Olympus [oh–LIM–pes]: the highest mountain in Greece; its peak is home to all the major gods, except for my brother, Po, and me.

Naxos [NAK-sos]: an island in the Aegean Sea, where Ariadne and I were put ashore by Theseus.

Naiads [NIGH–ads]: water nymphs.

nectar [NECK-ter]: what we gods like to drink to make us look good and feel godly.

nymph [NIMF]: any of various female nature spirits.

oracle [OR-uh-kul]: a sacred place where sibyls are said to foretell the future; sibyls and their prophesies are sometimes called oracles.

Pasiphae [pah-SIF-uh-ee]: Queen of Crete; wife of King Minos, and mother of the Minotaur.

Persephone [per-SEF-uh-knee]: goddess of spring and my Queen of the Underworld. The Romans call her **Proserpina**.

Poseidon [po-SIGH-den]: my bro Po; god of the seas, rivers, lakes, and earthquakes; one of the XII Power Olympians; actual father of Theseus by his short-term wife, Aethra. The Romans call him **Neptune**.

Procrustes [pro-CRUST-eez]: giant bully of ancient Greece who stretched or shortened mortals to fit into his long or short iron beds.

Psyche [SIGH-key]: a mortal princess loved by Cupid; her name means "soul."

Python [PIE-thon]: a huge serpent who guarded the Oracle of Delphi; also known as a champion wrestler.

Roman numerals: what the ancients used instead of counting on their fingers.

I	1	XI	11	XXX	30
II	2	XII	12	XL	40
III	3	XIII	13	L	50
IV	4	XIV	14	LX	60
V	5	XV	15	LXX	70
VI	6	XVI	16	LXXX	80
VII	7	XVII	17	XC	90
VIII	8	XVIII	18	C	100
IX	9	XIX	19	D	500
X	10	XX	20	M	1000

Sciron [SKY-ron]: giant bully of ancient Greece who kicked his victims off a cliff to a huge sea turtle waiting below.

Scorpion [SKOR-pee-un]: monstrous arachnid with venom in its tail; a wrestling phenom fated to be immortalized as a starry constellation.

sibyl [SIB-ul]: a mortal woman said to be able to foretell the future; a prophetess.

Sinis [SIGH-nis]: a giant bully of ancient Greece

who tied his victims to bent-over pine trees and catapulted them to their deaths.

Talos [TAL-os]: a huge bronze robot made by Hephaestus to guard the shores of Knossus.

Tartarus [TAR-tar-us]: the deepest pit in the Underworld and home of the Punishment Fields, where burning flames and red hot lava eternally torment the ghosts of the wicked.

Thalia [THA-lee-uh]: daughter of Zeus and muse of comedy.

Thebes [THEEBZ]: city in Greece; home of Wrestle Dome.

Theseus [THEE-see-us]: a great hero of ancient Athens who is known for never taking the easy way out and, mistakenly, for slaying the Minotaur.

Tisi see **Furies**.

Troezen [TREE-zen]: city in the Peloponnese; birthplace of Theseus.

Underworld: my very own kingdom, where the ghosts of dead mortals come to spend eternity.

Zeus [ZOOS]: rhymes with *goose*, which pretty much says it all; my little brother, a major myth-o-maniac and a cheater, who managed to set himself up as Ruler of the Universe. The Romans call him **Jupiter**.